T0375747

# THE UNDEFEATED

Paul Colella

iUniverse, Inc.
Bloomington

The Undefeated



iUniverse books may be ordered through booksellers or by contacting:

iUniverse
1663 Liberty Drive
Bloomington, IN 47403
www.iuniverse.com
1-800-Authors (1-800-288-4677)



ISBN: 978-1-4620-1790-4 (sc)
ISBN: 978-1-4620-1792-8 (hc)
ISBN: 978-1-4620-1791-1 (e)

Printed in the United States of America

iUniverse rev. date: 5/13/2011

In memory of Mae Knobloch—a wonderful neighbor and loyal fan.
and
To Frances Selmecki—a remarkable woman,
who loves and inspires unconditionally.

# Chapter I

For one moment more, Dr. Thomas Gage stood at his makeshift operating table with a scalpel in the palm of his hand. The steel of the blade was winking in the candlelight like a cold, slanted eye. It was at this familiar moment that he wished with all his heart that he had never elected to follow the surgeon's trade in peace or in war. It was early March of 1763, and war was taking a toll on the colonists and British soldiers fighting the French and their Indian allies in North America.

The young soldier was lying still on the table while Thomas began to make a careful incision along his patient's shoulder blade. This fresh-cheeked youth of no more than eighteen years of age had been struck down in the shadow of England's flag after two years of fighting the French and their Indian allies. He was the son of General Victor Kent, a prominent and high-ranking officer in the British army.

The British officers, observing protocol rigidly, still stood at dress parade along the clay-chinked wall while the candlelight was striking brightness from collar tabs and polished buttons. General Kent, unable to bear witness to his son's operation, remained nearby, concealed in the shadows of the camp.

Balancing the scalpel between his thumb and forefinger, Thomas continued to cut the skin while blood slowly leaked from the wound. Thomas was determined to remove the bullet and all fragments from his young patient's shoulder.

"The bullet appears to be deeply embedded, and therefore I must dig deep to remove it," said Thomas.

"Dr. Gage, you are a skillful surgeon, and your patient is in good hands," replied Jack, the doctor's orderly. "He's a strong young ox with a good chance of survival."

Thomas shifted his fingers while pressing hard to control excessive bleeding. Deep in the wound the bullet was lodged, but Thomas's careful cutting enabled him to dig out the foreign object and its remnants. Once the bullet had been removed, the good doctor controlled the bleeding with tight compresses that eventually diminished the stream of blood to a slow trickle. When he had set the final dressing to the wound, he stepped away from the table and thought to himself that a blend of knowledge and luck had saved a life. Although the general's son had survived the operation, Thomas was concerned about the possibility of infection setting in. Unfortunately, Thomas had witnessed many patients surviving under the knife but succumbing to infection days later.

When General Kent had received word that the operation had been completed, he approached Thomas and expressed his undying gratitude for saving his son's life. Thomas replied by telling the general it was his trade to save lives, whether they be friend or foe. He also informed the general that a watchful eye must keep vigil for the first sign of infection. Then Thomas politely excused himself while the general went to be with his son.

When Thomas returned to his quarters, he warmed himself by the fire on the open fieldstone hearth that made his cramped room warm and cozy. Almost no wind could find its way between the well-stacked logs. Once rid of the chills of the night, he lit his desk candle from the hearth, sat down at a small table, and began to enter the details of the operation in his journal. After writing for some time, he raised his head and stared into the flames of the fire while pondering in his mind how many more lives would become guests at death's door before this dreadful war would end.

---

Meanwhile, the next day, across the Atlantic Ocean in the city of London, a very intense trial was taking place in the King's Criminal

Court. No one spoke, no one moved, and silence, accompanied by the presence of doom and gloom, filled the courtroom. The judge, Sir Henry Barton, sat with his robes of office drawn tightly around him and his powdered wig pulled low on his forehead as he wondered why the most difficult cases were always assigned to him. The trial that was coming to an end had been particularly trying. Sir Henry felt unhappy as he often did when he was about to pass sentence. He gave a sigh and then rapped his gavel on the bench and raised his head.

"The prisoner will stand before the bar," he said.

Major Richard Hayes, dressed in the full-dress scarlet and white uniform of an officer of the Royal Army, stood and walked to the front of the courtroom. He was tall and rugged, and his clean-cut features and mesmerizing blue eyes showed determination and courage. His dark hair, which he wore tied with a ribbon at the back of his neck, was neatly brushed, his uniform was spotless, and he carried himself with dignity.

There was a stir among the female spectators, who turned to each other, whispering. These women, who attended trials for the purpose of recreation, had long been in agreement that Major Richard Hayes was one of the most personable and handsome prisoners they had ever seen.

Some of the male spectators felt sympathy for the major and agreed that he had been guilty of poor judgment but had not committed a heinous crime; however, a group of men in the front rows reserved for witnesses looked upon him with contempt and bitterness, as evident on their faces.

"Have you anything to say for yourself before this court pronounces judgment?" asked Sir Henry.

"Milord Justice, I have acted as my own solicitor-at-law in this trial, and I beg leave to review certain facts," replied Richard in a firm voice. "When I first met the colonial, Theodore Blakeslee, early this year, he convinced me that the financial venture on which he was to embark was sound. When he told me he proposed to buy land from the government of Massachusetts Bay Colony at one shilling per acre and sell it to immigrants to the colony at five shillings per acre, I believed him. I'm still not completely convinced that he hasn't done what he said he would."

"Unfortunately, Mr. Blakeslee is not here to tell his side of the story, and the law does not permit the extradition of colonials to testify in cases of this sort," declared Sir Henry.

Then he informed Major Hayes to continue. The major went on to say that he suspected Blakeslee of being a swindler.

"Theodore Blakeslee has answered none of the many letters I have written to him since he returned to Boston nearly ten months ago. Perhaps I was wrong to persuade my friends and associates to invest their savings in Blakeslee's company. But I sincerely thought the investment was sound, and I was trying to share my own good fortune with them. I would like to remind this court that I myself gave Blakeslee four thousand pounds, which is the total amount I inherited when my parents died."

Sir Henry leaned over the bench and stared intently at the major, and then asked him to state the motives for making this investment.

"I was looking for a good return on my investment, because I was interested in buying myself an estate that would be supported by tenant farmers. After ten years of fighting as a professional soldier, I wanted to lead an existence that had meaning by settling down, meeting a young woman who felt as I did, marrying, and raising a family," confessed Richard.

He explained that he found Blakeslee's arguments very convincing, and Blakeslee himself was investing his own funds in the land company as well. Thousands of newcomers were arriving in New England every month, Blakeslee had told him, and all of them wanted farms of their own.

"I am very sorry for making a terrible call in judgment and for trusting a man who looked and talked like a gentleman but was actually a scoundrel in disguise. I have acted in good faith, and my own loss has been greater by far than that of any of my friends. If I had two or three thousand pounds, I'd gladly repay them. Regardless of the outcome of this trial, I consider that sum a debt of honor that I will accumulate for them in one way or another. I have no more to say, Milord Justice," declared a repentant Richard, who stood tall while holding his plumed hat rigidly under his left arm.

Sir Henry picked up a pile of several letters from the bench and explained to those present in the courtroom that the letters were written by fellow army officers and officials as well as some of London's prominent members of society who spoke of the major's accomplishments and good deeds as a soldier and a civilian. After reading excerpts from a few of the letters, Sir Henry reflected a few moments in silence and then spoke.

"Since the accused, Major Richard Hayes, has exhausted his own funds and is not able to repay his friends and associates for their losses, this court must sentence the prisoner to New Gate Prison as a debtor for a term not to exceed more than twenty years," said a stern Sir Henry.

Spectators in the crowd gasped upon hearing the judge's harsh sentence. Those in the front row smiled with a devilish delight while an unmoved Major Hayes stood erect with a blank expression on his face.

Sir Henry demanded silence as he lowered his gavel on the bench. When all was quiet, he addressed the major by telling him that the court had taken into consideration his long and faithful service to the Crown and that he was indeed a man of honor who was deceived by an unscrupulous individual. Sir Henry then told the major that within the limitations permitted to him by law and at his discretion, he would temper justice with mercy.

"Therefore, Richard Hayes, I suspend judgment until one year from today. This court gives you twelve months to repay those persons whom you persuaded to invest money with Theodore Blakeslee. If that is accomplished, it will be the pleasure of this court to dismiss all charges against you. If not, you will be sentenced to debtor's prison with a more extended sentence than the previously pronounced. The King's Criminal Court stands adjourned," replied Sir Henry as he lowered his gavel on the bench.

The spectators slowly left the courtroom while Richard Hayes remained behind.

---

A sharp March wind filled the sails of the ship that made its way south toward Boston, along the shore of Nova Scotia. Standing on the ship's deck was Richard Hayes, dressed in an inexpensive wool coat with fingers numb from the cold. As he put one hand deep in his pocket, he touched the few remaining gold coins that stood between him and starvation. He stared sadly at the land in the nearby distance, and he wondered if he would have been wiser to remain in England

and earn enough money to repay his friends and associates. But he had convinced himself that only by coming to the New World could he truly establish his innocence and clear his name.

# Chapter 2

Richard was determined to go to Boston, seek out and confront Theodore Blakeslee in person, and insist on the return of the full amount of money he and his friends had given the swindler. He had whipped himself into a spirit of renewed strength but had not realized how thoroughly unpleasant it would be to put the plan into operation. He had taken passage on the *Lonesome Mermaid*, a colonial ship, for only one reason: it had been the cheapest available. His tiny cabin was crowded and inadequate, and the long weeks at sea had been the loneliest and most boring time of his life.

He was the ship's only passenger, so he had been forced to spend time in the company of the various crew members, who were very unpolished, vulgar, and crude in their mannerism and speech. The ship's master, Isaac Brown, who was nearly the same age as Richard, was stern in appearance and very quiet. He only engaged in conversation about the good fortunes that could be made in New England. Isaac's stories of wealth and success reminded Richard of the way that Theodore Blakeslee had spoken.

As Richard stared out at the rolling, gray-green sea, he sensed the approach of someone behind him. Half-turning, he saw a frail sailor with a small scar on his left cheek coming toward him. The sailor's name was Joshua Pierce. It was too late for Richard to escape, so he resigned himself to the fact that he had to speak with the sailor.

"Well, there she is," Joshua exclaimed while waving his bony hand in the general direction of the shore. "Some call it the land of milk and honey, just like God had promised the children of Israel under the leadership of Moses as they made their flight out of Egypt. As the story goes, the Israelites did not appreciate God's generosity, and consequently suffered for their sins and foolishness."

Richard glanced in the direction of the hills and saw a desolate and uninhabited area that was blanketed by a covering of wet snow. The landscape made for a bleak and pathetic first impression. When Richard inquired if this was New England, Joshua laughed and then explained that it was not New England but still Nova Scotia, and that it was called Arcadia before the British took it over from the French.

"This is very good, rich country for folks to settle down in," replied Joshua. "The day is coming soon when this whole province will be filled with people growing crops and raising livestock while its two chief towns, Annapolis Royal and Canton, will be busting out at their sides with inhabitants."

As far as Richard was concerned, he would be content never to set his eyes on any part of Nova Scotia again. All that really interested him was reaching Boston and finding Theodore Blakeslee. Anxious to reach his destination, Richard asked Joshua how many more days it would be until they reached Boston. Joshua replied by telling him that since the captain was going straight through without stopping at any ports, they would be in Boston within three days.

Richard was surprised but pleased that they were so close to their destination. The voyage had seemed endless that he had lost all concept of time. But now he was excited with the realization that in another seventy-two hours he might be facing Theodore Blakeslee. Eager to verify the information he had just been told, he hurried to find the captain. He found him on the other side of the ship, but the captain was preoccupied with a handful of crewmen who were watching a small floating vessel drifting aimlessly near the *Lonesome Mermaid*. Her sail had been torn, and waves were washing over her little deck as she bobbed up and down in the water. The captain gave the order to head straight for the small vessel that seemed to be unmanned.

As Richard and the captain stared from over the railing of the ship, they saw someone on the vessel's deck clinging to the mast with one hand and trying without success to untangle a snarled, wet line with the other.

When the *Lonesome Mermaid* was no more than one hundred yards from the boat, the captain ordered his crewmen to lower a rescue boat and bring in the floating vessel. The oarsmen in the rescue boat held their boat steady while one man threw a line around the mast of the small vessel. Then the transfer of the passengers of the small vessel was made onto the rescue boat. There was a man dressed in farm attire, a small boy wearing a straw hat, and a young woman with long, dark hair. After the transfer was completed, the rescue boat headed back to the *Lonesome Mermaid* with the vessel in tow.

Richard watched closely from over the railing of the ship and noticed that the young woman, although her appearance seemed unkempt, was very pretty. The ends of her hair were wet and matted, but her features looked attractive and feminine, and her green eyes were appealing. She was wearing a long dress of thick, coarsely woven wool that looked particularly dreadful, but its wetness against her body revealed a figure that was little short of perfect, with broad shoulders and a small waist.

It was evident that the young woman, along with the man and little boy, had undergone a terrible experience, but all three seemed calm when they finally stood on the ship's deck. The captain ordered two of the sailors to bring blankets, and then introduced himself to his newly found passengers.

The little boy clung to the leg of the man in farm attire, who introduced themselves as Roger Simmons and his son, Seth. The young woman cordially smiled and then told everyone her name was Nancy Graham. Shivering, she welcomed a warm blanket and wrapped it around her body. She looked at the men, including Richard, who had gathered around the three of them, and then spoke with great emotion.

"The French have raided the town of Annapolis Royal without warning. They killed the men and took the women and children as prisoners before burning the entire town to the ground. We three are the only survivors."

# Chapter 3

Wrapped in heavy blankets, Nancy Graham sat in the captain's quarters and told the captain and Richard her horrific story while sipping hot rum-laced tea from a mug. She explained that she had been visiting the Simmons' farm and checking in on Roger, who was grieving the loss of his wife, who had died three months earlier. As they walked about the farm, they saw smoke from in the nearby distance and heard gunshots and loud screams. Roger hurried to the top of a hill overlooking his farm, and to his horror, saw French soldiers attacking the town. He quickly hurried down the hill and took hold of Seth and Nancy, and they retreated through the woods. When they reached an isolated cove, he untied one of two small fishing boats that was the property of his neighbors and then ushered Nancy and his son onto the small vessel and sailed away.

As the boat made its way to the open water, Nancy watched in astonishment and horror as the French fleet opened a violent bombardment of the town, systematically destroying merchant ships in the harbor and burning buildings in the town. Hundreds of uniformed Frenchmen had come ashore in boats and began a massive raid upon the settlement's inhabitants. Nancy explained vehemently that loud screams of the innocent being attacked and the sight of smoke and fire would remain etched in her mind forever.

They had hoped to sail to one of the smaller villages farther down the coast, but Roger's inadequate knowledge of boats had caused them to drift out into the ocean. They had been drifting aimlessly for at least a few hours until the *Lonesome Mermaid* had rescued them. After finishing her story, Nancy held back tears and sat quietly staring into space.

Richard and the captain left Nancy and went to check on Roger Simmons and his son in another cabin. When questioned by the captain, Roger gave an exact account of what had happened that was similar to what Nancy had said. Roger sat in a wooden chair, keeping a close eye on his son, who was wrapped in several blankets and sleeping on a cot.

After leaving Roger and his son, the captain gave orders to sail into the harbor. He wanted to see for himself just how severe the damage to Annapolis Royal had been, and he wanted to search for other survivors. The captain was hoping that Nancy was mistaken and others had also escaped the French and were now wandering around the ruins in need of assistance. Richard hurried to his cabin, put on his sword, loaded his pistol, and placed it in his belt.

For the present, Richard was not thinking about the urgency to reach Boston and find Theodore Blakeslee. It was shocking beyond belief that the French had attacked an undefended town without first breaking diplomatic relations. Perhaps it was because the peace treaty that officially ended the French and Indian War in the New World had not been signed or news of peace negotiations had not yet reached the proper authorities. Whatever the reason, the French were not justified in their brutal attack upon a helpless town.

When Richard returned to the deck, he saw that the *Lonesome Mermaid* had sailed closer to the shoreline and was moving past thick weeds. Then the ship came to a clearing near the far end of the harbor. As he stared at the sight before him, the destruction made him feel numb from sorrow and anger. All that was left of a once thriving and prosperous town was a large area of rubble and ruins. Only the docks were intact. All the homes, shops, warehouses, and other buildings were charred shells. Richard and the crew viewed the devastation in grim solace.

After anchoring the ship alongside a wharf, the captain assigned men in pairs to diligently search the town for survivors. At that moment, Nancy appeared on deck and said she felt strong enough to accompany the men ashore. She insisted on going, and Richard volunteered to escort her. The captain did not refuse her request.

They went ashore with Nancy leading the way. She was very pale and did not speak as she held her head high while glancing to the right and then the left. Richard felt great sympathy for her and wanted to comfort her, but he knew that nothing he could say would help her, so he remained silent. They walked past a row of burnt warehouses, and after peeking through a broken window, Richard realized that nothing of value remained. The French had taken all supplies before withdrawing and leaving a path of destruction behind them.

"Those French are barbarians. They need to pay for this atrocity. I swear upon my last dying breath to avenge the people of this once beloved town," cried a pitiful Nancy as she walked through the ruins.

"Like it tells us in Deuteronomy, vengeance belongs to the Lord," said Joshua Pierce in a loud voice. "I am a man of peace, but I will not be satisfied until there is not one Frenchman left in all of North America."

As they continued to walk through the destroyed town, they saw more charred buildings as well as corpses of men, women, and even a few children scattered about. One, in particular, was an older man who had attempted to defend his home, and still clutched his musket in his hand. After searching for several hours, everyone agreed that there were no survivors and nothing of value to claim, so they decided to return to the ship. Annapolis Royal was inhabited now only by ghosts.

Upon hearing the news, Nancy asked the captain if they could go to her home so she could examine the ruins and search for anything that may have survived the fires. The captain agreed, and the men allowed her to lead the way down a narrow path that took them to her two-story home, which had broken windows but was not charred like many of the other homes and buildings.

Nancy entered through the broken front door and hurried to a first-floor bedroom, where she struggled to remove a large trunk. Richard came to her assistance, and she opened the lid and rummaged through gowns and other female apparel that was stored inside. After carefully examining the contents, she asked permission of the captain to bring the trunk aboard the ship. The captain agreed and motioned to his men to take the trunk. Nancy then went over to a secret panel in the wall, which was hidden behind a sofa. She opened the panel and removed a leather box. Holding the box tightly in her hands, she informed Richard and the captain that it was time to leave.

As they approached the docks, it was quite evident to all in the search party that Nancy Graham, Roger Simmons, and his son, Seth, were the only survivors of Annapolis Royal. Nancy, still clutching the box in one hand, placed her other hand on Richard's shoulder and began to sigh. Then she took a deep breath and gazed out at the sea as tears filled her eyes. Richard looked at her, thinking that at last she would weep, but Nancy surprised him.

"It is good to be leaving this place of death and destruction. I am not sorry to go," she uttered as she walked down the long wharf to the *Lonesome Mermaid.*

These words of insensitivity gave Richard a strange feeling, and at that moment he began to have uncomfortable feelings about Nancy. He surmised that perhaps there was another side to this lovely woman, a side that was unattractive and uncompassionate.

# Chapter 4

After four days of battling rough seas and stormy weather, the *Lonesome Mermaid* arrived safely in the port of Boston. Boston was the first major city in the American colonies with a population of more than thirty thousand people. The grim, forbidding spirits of Increase and Cotton Mather no longer hovered over the community; graduates of Harvard College were recognized as young men of great learning, and the city was, in every sense, the center of colonial life.

Boston Harbor was crowded with merchants and tradesmen conducting a lively trade with Europe and the West Indies. Small factories and shops were producing a variety of goods. Farmers, not only from Massachusetts Bay but also from Connecticut, New Hampshire, and the District of Maine, brought their wares and produce to the markets of Boston. Progress in the construction of new homes and public buildings was evident throughout the city. In the shipyards, men worked day and night to build ships that would bear proud testimony to the skill of Boston shipwrights when they were on the high seas. Several weekly newspapers were circulated throughout the city, including a newcomer called *The Independent Advertiser* that was not considered very respectable because of its fiery and outspoken editor, Samuel Adams.

Two companies of regular English troops were stationed in the city to maintain law and order and protect the city and its ports from invaders.

As Richard and the others left the ship, they could hear church bells ringing in the distance. The captain went to the royal governor's office to file his account of what had happened at Annapolis Royal. Roger Simmons and his son, as well as Nancy Graham, went with the captain to give their eye-witness testimony.

Before leaving the ship, Nancy inquired about a place to take up lodging. The captain was gracious to advise her that a suitable place for a young lady like herself would be Hancock's Inn. He also had two sailors deliver her trunk of belongings to the inn. Richard, due to his financial situation, took lodging at a more modest place, the Fairview Tavern, down the street from Hancock's Inn.

After settling into his room upstairs from the tavern, Richard went downstairs to partake in a delicious meal of chicken with corn, cucumber, lettuce, and string beans, and a mug of ale.

The tavern owner was a short and chubby man with rosy cheeks, whose round belly would move up and down when he laughed.

After enjoying his meal, Richard decided to take a tour of some of Boston's sights. As he walked along the cobblestone streets, he was impressed by the houses, especially those on Beacon Hill, which stood three stories high and were painted white and had real glass in their windows. These homes were quite elegant and resembled the fine and mighty establishments near St. James' Palace in London.

After spending some time getting acquainted with certain parts of the city, Richard decided to pay a call to Nancy Graham at Hancock's Inn. When he arrived at the inn, one of Boston's prominent citizens, William Wentworth, was sitting in the common room with his wife, waiting to see Nancy. A few moments later, an elegantly dressed Nancy came down the stairs to meet her guests. William and his wife, Georgiana, greeted Nancy graciously and explained that they were very good friends of the governor. They had come to pay their respects and offer their sympathy regarding the ordeal that Nancy had experienced at Annapolis Royal. Mrs. Wentworth, with her husband's consent, invited Nancy to stay with them for as long as she wished. Both Mr. and Mrs. Wentworth believed that Nancy would be more comfortable at their home, with servants to assist her, than in a lonely room at a local inn.

Nancy was very grateful, and after staring at a surprised Richard, who was standing in the corner of the common room, agreed to accept the Wentworth's hospitality. Mr. and Mrs. Wentworth were delighted with her acceptance and told Nancy that they would wait for her in their carriage.

After the couple had left, Nancy went up to Richard and thanked him for the kindness and companionship he had extended when they had walked among the ruins of Annapolis Royal.

"Thank you for being with me during a horrible time in my life," she said. "I have lost my home, my servants, and many of my precious belongings, but I have survived, and I shall put this awful tragedy behind me and start living again," said Nancy with a smile. "Please, come and visit me at the Wentworth's home. I am certain you will be welcomed there."

Richard smiled at the beautiful young woman and wished her well. He then reached out for her hand and gently kissed it. Before he departed, he took a moment to stare into her attractive green eyes while she gazed into his mesmerizing blue ones. Both appeared to be in a trance with one another. Their moment of intense pleasure was interrupted when a group of tradesmen entered the room, looking for a place to rest from their tiresome journey. Acting as a gentleman, Richard escorted Nancy outside to the waiting carriage.

As the carriage pulled away, he watched as it disappeared into the distance while thinking that this beautiful woman who had survived a harrowing ordeal had fascinated him so much that he could not get her out of his mind. He decided to renew their acquaintance in the near future, but first he had to begin his search for Theodore Blakeslee and clear his good name.

Richard walked down the street, past several red brick buildings. As he made his way back to the Fairview Tavern, he was unaware that someone dressed in a dark blue cloak was following him.

# Chapter 5

Dr. Thomas Gage was relaxing in the drawing room at Huntington Hall. He was enjoying a glass of sherry while partaking in the solace and delight of being at home. He did not miss the brutal elements of the untamed frontier or his stay at Fort Wilderness.

Thomas went to sit in a Chippendale chair at the large mahogany desk, where he took hold of a fresh quill that was beside the inkpot. He opened his journal and began to write.

*I have saved the lives of several young soldiers in the British army who had fought bravely to protect the colonists from the French and their Indian allies. Both France and England are determined to push the other out of the rich Ohio Valley. The British army, under the leadership of General Edward Braddock, vowed to destroy Fort Duquesne and to win the war quickly.*

*Despite Britain's determination to fight, inadequate planning and insufficient funding had slowed the British war effort, causing the war to last a period of seven years. I am hopeful that once a peace treaty has been signed there will be no more bloodshed, but realistically I know that as long as man is capable of inhumanity toward his brother, war and death are inevitable, especially when it comes to centuries of animosity between the English and the French.*

Thomas's solitude and writing were interrupted by the arrival of his mother, Martha Huntington Gage, whose father was the founder and first occupant of Huntington Hall. Martha was an elegantly dressed woman who wore the latest fashions from London and paid close attention to protocol and the rules of propriety while ensuring she kept company with only prominent citizens of Boston's high society.

She was elated that her son safely returned home from Fort Wilderness. However, she was a bit distressed about the fact that he was still a bachelor at the age of twenty-six and devoting his life to the medical profession.

"My dear son, I am most grateful that you have returned home safely," she said. "I hope and pray that this wretched war will soon end and you will not be making excursions to forts deep in untamed territories, administering to wounded and dying soldiers while exposing your own life to danger. I would prefer that you concentrate your attention on finding a wife, getting married, and giving me an heir to carry on the Gage legacy."

Thomas smiled at his mother as he closed the journal and said, "My dear mother, you can always be counted upon for planning my future."

Then he explained to her that his attentions were focused on medicine and healing the sick. For the present, he was happy and content with his life just the way it was. Martha was not pleased with her son's response, but she carefully hid her objections. She decided not to engage in an argument, but instead to enjoy Thomas's homecoming, so she joined her son in a glass of sherry and then they went into the dining room for supper.

---

The loud roar of musketry that had echoed across the plains of the untamed wilderness for several years had finally ceased. The French had been defeated. General James Wolfe was laying on a cot in his tent, slowly dying from the wounds he had received in a battle with his adversary, the Marquis de Montcalm, on the Plains of Abraham. Unbeknownst to General Wolfe, the marquis had already succumbed to death from the wounds of that battle, and the general was currently fighting a battle to maintain every last breath of life.

As he was dying, he called for his trusted friend Lord Jeffrey Amherst, to be by his side. He ordered everyone, including his physician and male servant, to leave his presence. Once the general was alone with Lord Amherst, he instructed his friend to go to the desk in the corner, open the top drawer, and remove a letter sealed in an envelope.

"When I am gone from this world, I want you to deliver that letter to the person whose name is written on the envelope. The person you will seek is presently in Boston. Make certain that only that person receives the letter and no one else. It is very important that my wishes are carried out. The letter contains a powerful secret that must be protected at any cost," uttered a dying General Wolfe.

Lord Amherst assured his friend that he would carry out his wishes. Then he walked over to a small table and poured a glass of water and brought it to the general, who refused to take a drink.

"The French have been defeated. Now, God be praised, I will die in peace," said General Wolfe.

And then he took his last breath before expiring, with his eyes looking up at the sky.

Lord Amherst, holding back tears, closed the eyes of his dead friend, and replied, "The mighty general is no more." Then he took the bed quilt and covered the dead general's face.

---

In Boston, an exhausted Richard had returned to his room upstairs from the Fairview Tavern. A large crowd of tradesmen and merchants were gathered downstairs, drinking wine and ale, while celebrating the end of the war and discussing plans for the expansion of settlement into the Ohio Valley. Richard, who was not interested in what was taking place downstairs, removed his black boots and sat down in a comfortable chair while contemplating his plan of finding Theodore Blakeslee. Soon a wave of sleep slowly enveloped him, and he found it difficult to keep his eyes open. After struggling for some time, sleep finally won out, and Richard closed his eyes while sitting upright in the chair.

The room was dark, and all was silent except for the faint sound of voices coming from down in the common room. Suddenly, the door to his room slowly and quietly opened while an unsuspecting Richard remained sleeping in his chair. Someone had entered the room and was making his way toward Richard. But the sound of a squeaky floor board caused him to open his eyes. To his horror, he suddenly felt two strong hands clenched around his throat.

# Chapter 6

Richard struggled to remove the hands from his throat as he gasped for air. He tried desperately to rise from his chair, but his masked attacker held him in his place, determined to kill him. As the two continued to struggle, their confrontation was abruptly interrupted by the tavern owner's wife, who came into the room carrying a tray of food. Upon seeing what was taking place, the woman screamed from fright and dropped the tray.

The woman's unexpected arrival and harsh screams caused the attacker to flee the room. Richard took a few moments to catch his breath, and then hurried frantically after his attacker. By the time he made his way downstairs, the intruder had managed to blend in with the large crowd. Richard was shouting in the common room as he searched for his attacker. Several people, disturbed by the chaos, asked what was going on. The crowded room and confusion made it convenient for the attacker to escape. A frustrated and agitated Richard gave up the search, and then went back upstairs, where he found the woman cleaning up the food that had spilled from the tray. She appeared to be extremely frightened, especially since she was a very timid person, who was tall and bony with an angular face. Her husband and neighbors had referred to her as being scared of her own shadow. Richard was grateful for her intrusion and helped her clean up the debris.

The tavern owner soon joined them and demanded an explanation of what had happened. Richard told him that someone tried to kill him, and the tavern owner's wife verified his story. The tavern owner insisted that Richard go to the authorities and report the attempt on his life. To satisfy the chubby old man, Richard agreed to go to see the constable in the morning.

"I am certain that whoever came here will not be returning tonight. I will make a report to the constable tomorrow. I am exhausted, so I wish to be alone. Thank you for your concern and kindness," replied Richard.

The tavern owner and his wife left their guest and returned downstairs to their customers in the common room. Richard closed the door behind him and began to ponder, wondering who would want to kill him and why. As he reflected and agonized over these questions, only one name came to mind, and it was Theodore Blakeslee. Richard wondered if it had been Theodore, how had he known where to find him? Richard realized that if the attacker was indeed Theodore, then the swindler, who had stolen from him and his friends, was not only a thief but a very dangerous scoundrel.

The next morning after breakfast, Richard went to the constable's office along with the tavern owner's wife. The constable listened intensely to their story. He made some notes before asking Richard why someone would want to harm him and if he had any thoughts about the identity of his attacker. Richard kept his thoughts about Theodore and his situation to himself. Before dismissing them, the constable informed him to be careful. Richard escorted the tavern owner's wife back to her husband's establishment, and then he went upstairs and took hold of the pistol he had stored in a desk drawer. He placed the pistol under his coat and went on his way to seek out Theodore Blakeslee.

---

At Huntington Hall, while Martha Gage was sitting in the drawing room having a cup of tea, admiring the beautiful furnishings and ornate chandelier, she was overcome by feelings of loneliness as she still missed her beloved husband who had died nearly five years ago. He had been her best friend, confidant, and partner, and they had shared two wonderful children, Thomas and Cassandra. Thomas was for now content with remaining a bachelor, and Cassandra was living in England with her husband, and Martha was longing for an extension to her family tree.

After finishing her tea, she took a turn about the room, but her small constitution was interrupted by the housekeeper, Mrs. Fitch, who announced the arrival of Georgiana Wentworth and her companion, Nancy Graham. Martha was delighted to see her dear friend Georgiana, and smiled graciously as she greeted her guests. Martha was particularly interested in making Nancy Graham's acquaintance.

"My dear Martha, let me introduce to you the lovely Nancy Graham. She is the woman who survived that horrid experience at Annapolis Royal. She is residing with William and me at our home," said Georgiana.

"It is a pleasure to meet you, Mrs. Gage. You have a magnificent home," said Nancy with a smile.

"The pleasure is all mine, my dear. I am so glad that you and Georgiana have called upon me. Please, sit down and make yourselves comfortable."

Martha played the gracious hostess by offering a cup of tea to her guests, and then the women engaged in polite and petty conversation. Nancy was not shy in talking about herself. She told an attentive Martha and Georgiana that she was an only child and that both her parents were deceased. After her parents' death, she inherited a sum of five thousand pounds a year, and she left England and had been living very comfortably in her home in Annapolis Royal for several years before the town was destroyed by the vicious French. She also said that she was not married as was evident by no wedding ring on her finger, and she had a desire to settle down with a man of good fortune and character, and have a family.

"Family is very important, especially for the survival of one's family name," said Nancy. "I seem to be enjoying Boston very much, and I'm considering making it my new home, thanks to the friendly persuasion and hospitality of Mr. and Mrs. Wentworth."

The women's conversation was interrupted by Thomas's arrival home. When he entered the room, Georgiana was delighted to see him and rose from her chair to embrace him.

Nancy was carefully examining Thomas from head to toe and was pleased by what she saw. Thomas had broad shoulders with a strong build, and dark hair with eyes to match. He was rich, an elegant dresser, and a fine gentleman who would catch the eye of any available woman.

Georgiana made the introductions, and there seemed to be a connection between Thomas and Nancy. Thomas decided to stay and visit while having a cup of tea, much to his mother's chagrin. Martha remained quiet but observant as she watched her son partake in conversation with her friend Georgiana and her captivating companion Nancy Graham, who seemed taken with Thomas. As she stared at Nancy and her attractive but seductive appearance, Martha suddenly had a disturbing feeling that the glare of Nancy's green eyes reminded her of the devil's disciple. But she remained the gracious hostess while anxiously anticipating Georgiana and Nancy's departure.

---

While walking the streets of Boston searching for Theodore Blakeslee, Richard became seemingly discouraged in his futile effort to locate the swindler. The sky became gray, and it began to rain. A cold wind hissed against his cheeks. As he walked along the side of the street, he caught a glimpse of a young woman carrying a bundle in her arms while attempting to cross the street. The woman appeared to be more preoccupied with what she had in her hands than where she was going. Suddenly, a coach came from around the corner and was heading right toward the unsuspecting woman. Richard shouted for her to get out of the way, but she did not listen. Realizing that she was about to be hit by the fast-approaching coach, Richard ran as quickly as he could into the street to rescue her. A loud, screeching sound accompanied by the galloping of horses was heard, and then all was quiet.

# Chapter 7

The coach had come to a complete halt, and the passengers inside were a bit shaken but unharmed, as was the driver.

Alongside the road, Richard removed himself from atop of the young woman who he had managed to shove out of harm's way. He helped her to her feet. She was a bit frightened from the ordeal but very grateful for Richard's quick thinking and intervention. Her petticoat was covered with dirt, and her lace cap had fallen off her head.

"Thank you for saving my life. Please forgive me for looking a fright," said the young woman in a sincere tone of voice. "My name is Sarah Dustin, and I am the daughter of George and Mabel Dustin."

"My name is Richard Hayes, and I am pleased to make your acquaintance despite these circumstances," replied Richard. "Are you all right? Should I fetch a doctor?"

"I am quite well, thanks to you."

Several spectators had gathered around Richard and Sarah, inquiring about their health. A man dressed in a finely tailored suit with gold buttons made his way through the crowd. Upon seeing Sarah, he embraced her and was relieved to see that she was unharmed. Sarah introduced the gentleman to Richard as her father, George Dustin. Mr. Dustin shook Richard's hand and thanked him wholeheartedly for saving his daughter's life.

"My Sarah is very much like her mother when it comes to shopping at the local shops and warehouses. They are always buying more than they can carry. I can speak for my wife when I say that we are in your debt for your selflessness and bravery in saving our precious daughter. I insist that you accompany my daughter and me to our home, where you will dine with us. It is the least we can do to show our gratitude," insisted George.

Having no prior engagements, Richard accepted the man's kind offer. The crowd of onlookers soon dissipated while Sarah and her father and Richard headed toward a waiting carriage around the corner. Unbeknownst to them, in the nearby distance, someone was watching them.

---

Nancy Graham was sitting on a soft divan in her bedroom at the Wentworth mansion. She was thinking about two men in particular. One was Richard Hayes, a man who was very personable and handsome with honorable intentions, but a commoner. The other gentleman, Thomas Gage, was handsome just like Richard, but a genteel sort of man with a kind spirit, an admirable profession, and a member of Boston's privileged class.

For Nancy, money always made a man most attractive, even if he had facial imperfections or an awkward physical appearance. But to her liking, Thomas Gage was both financially and physically handsome, and there was no doubt that he would make a fine husband. She was very pleased with the place where he resided and would be elated to have the opportunity of one day becoming mistress of Huntington Hall.

Nancy had realized that returning to Annapolis Royal was out of the question, and she could not take advantage of the Wentworth's hospitality indefinitely without people beginning to gossip. She decided that her only way to start a new life was to marry a man of fine fortune, and she felt that Thomas Gage was the right choice. While Nancy was planning a strategic move to become better acquainted with Thomas without revealing her true motives, a knock came at her door.

"Please come in," shouted Nancy.

"My dear Nancy, I hope that I am not disturbing you, but I come bearing good news," said Georgiana. "My husband, William, is going to give a ball here at the mansion in honor of the peace treaty between England and France, which will be signed in the next few months. It has been rumored that the French are giving up all their claims on this continent. This is certainly a time for celebration."

Upon hearing Georgiana's news about a ball, Nancy deviously calculated that this would be a perfect opportunity to be in Thomas Gage's company.

"Will you be inviting the Gage family to the ball?" Nancy asked.

"Martha Gage and her family are one of William's oldest and dearest friends. By all means, they will be invited, and I am certain that they will attend."

Once she heard Georgiana's response to her question, an elated Nancy rose from the sofa, embraced her friend, and told her that she had longed for a ball for quite some time. It was the perfect way to bring celebration and happiness after what had plagued the colonies these past seven years. Georgiana informed Nancy that they would go into town and shop for a gown to wear to the ball. Then she politely excused herself as she went to the kitchen to inquire about dinner.

After she was gone, Nancy moved about the room in a joyful manner, fantasizing that she and Thomas were dancing at the ball, dressed in their elegant attire, and being the envy of all those in attendance.

She then went over to the desk and took out the leather box that she had retrieved from the rubble of her home at Annapolis Royal. While gently rubbing the box, she whispered that everything was going to work out and she would eventually live happily ever after.

---

Upon his arrival at the Dustin estate, Richard was fascinated with the beautiful furnishings, the ornate chandeliers, the silk wallpaper, the magnificent portraits of the Dustin ancestors and relatives that hung in the great hall, and the elegant spiral staircase leading to the second floor.

*This is certainly a home of great beauty, elegance, and charm that would rival certain homes back in London,* thought Richard.

Mabel Dustin was a bit matronly, but charming and graceful in appearance. From what Richard could observe, Sarah had inherited her father's good looks more so than her mother's. Nonetheless, Sarah had a combination of both parents' personalities and good nature. Mabel was very grateful to Richard for saving her daughter, and was delighted that her husband had invited him to dine with them. She informed one of the servants to set another place at the table.

---

While Richard was enjoying the hospitality of the Dustin family, more than two hundred miles away at a small, northern settlement called Kingston, a full company of militia men were sworn in to protect the settlement from an impending Indian attack. Whenever men heard that their fellow colonists were in danger, they would pick up their muskets and leave their homes to go off to fight, regardless of the difficulties that their absence would cause. The women were left to manage the households and the farms while praying that their husbands would return home safely.

Seventy-five or more Huron warriors, dressed only in breechcloths and moccasins, their faces and shoulders daubed with broad streaks of paint, emerged from the woods and crept toward the east wall of the settlement. Each of the braves carried a musket and a long knife, but not a single shot was fired. It was the enemy's intent to make a surprise attack.

The man in charge of the militia was Sergeant Gordon Conroy. He made certain that the gates of Kingston were closed and properly secured. All colonists residing in the countryside were safely inside the walls. The women and children, along with the older men and women, crowded the local inn. The innkeeper's wife served hot cider and soup while the innkeeper made sure all the shutters were closed.

Sergeant Conroy gave orders to his men to hold their fire until the attackers were nearly upon the walls. He and his men waited patiently and quietly to fight while holding onto their muskets. As the Huron warriors inched closer to the wall, there was no hint from inside the settlement that the defenders suspected anything. When the long line of braves reached a position of no more than twelve feet from the wall, one of them called out a soft command. As soon as the command was given, the warriors rushed toward the wall, shouting a high-pitched war cry that echoed into the distance.

At that moment, the settlers and militia men opened fire from behind the wall. Every man selected his individual target and fired in unison. Their aim was accurate, and the Huron warriors were mowed down like a giant scythe. However, not all of the attackers had been struck down, and those who were still on their feet continued to race toward the wall.

Sergeant Conroy was surprised by the persistence and advancing of the warriors. After several minutes of musket shots, the few warriors who had survived fell back and retreated into the forest. Only a handful of the Huron had escaped. The ground outside the settlement was littered with the bodies of the dead, and silence filled the air.

The sergeant congratulated the men on their bravery and fine marksmanship. He then told them to remain alert and not to put their muskets down, for he believed that another attack may be possible.

"These savages are stubborn and unimaginative, and they will continue to attack until they win a battle, are driven off, or are annihilated. We must always be on our guard," replied a solemn Sergeant Conroy.

After addressing the men, he took a short respite by going to the inn for a hot meal and checking in on the colonists, who were lodging there temporarily.

Outside the walls, a Huron who had fallen among his dead warriors rose from the corpses and slowly and cautiously crawled undetected along the earthy ground. He managed to successfully conceal himself in a small, inconspicuous area not far from the front gate, and remained there in waiting.

# Chapter 8

**The next morning, Richard** was sitting in his room at the Fairview Inn, contemplating his next move in locating Theodore Blakeslee and trying to figure out if Blakeslee or someone else had made an attempt on his life a few nights ago.

As he sat pondering these thoughts, a knock came at the door. When Richard opened the door, George Dustin was standing in the doorway. He politely apologized for his unannounced visit, and he informed Richard that he had information regarding the whereabouts of Theodore Blakeslee.

"Please excuse the intrusion, my dear sir, but after our conversation last night concerning a certain unscrupulous individual, I felt that it was my obligation to come and tell you what I know," said a troubled George Dustin.

Richard invited him in and then closed the door. He offered George the only chair in the room while he sat adjacent on the bed and listened closely while his guest spoke. Surprisingly, George revealed to Richard that he was well acquainted with Theodore Blakeslee, and that he had sensed from their first encounter that Blakeslee was a man who was not to be trusted. However, Blakeslee had managed to use his charm, wit, and excellent manners to win the approval of his wife and the heart of his daughter.

"After you had confided in me the true purpose for being in Boston, and upon hearing the name Theodore Blakeslee, I knew in all good conscience that I had to reveal the truth to you. It is the least I can do after your courageous rescue of my beloved Sarah from the wheels of the coach," replied George.

He went on to say that Theodore was living quite comfortably in a house on Threadwell Street, and he had succeeded in becoming a member of Boston's high society thanks to the introduction and recommendation of his wife, Mabel.

"Tell me the location of Threadwell Street so I may go and call upon that scoundrel," replied Richard as he sprang from the bed. "It is imperative that I confront Theodore and make him confess to what he has done to me and assist me in clearing my name."

"I would have revealed the truth to you last night, but something was holding me back. After a sleepless night and an endless struggle with my conscience, I've come here today ready and eager to help you bring the man who has wronged you and your associates to justice."

Then George offered to accompany Richard to Theodore's home, but Richard insisted on going alone. George agreed to let Richard confront Theodore privately, but he was persistent in wanting to take him by carriage to Threadwell Street. Anxious to confront Theodore and realizing that George would not back down, Richard allowed George to take him there. Within a few minutes, both men were in the carriage and on their way.

---

Outside the gates of Kingston, Sergeant Conroy was instructing his soldiers, who were farmers and artisans ranging in age from about sixteen to mature citizens with gray hair, to bury the dead warriors in mass graves in the nearby woods. The other soldiers, with their muskets in hand, kept a watchful lookout for any Huron warriors.

While Conroy and his men were attending to their task at hand, three covered wagons filled with supplies had arrived at Kingston. After the wagons had been unloaded, Conroy and his men slowly made their departure. The first two wagons went through the front gate and down the dusty road, but the third wagon was detained while a handful of farmers loaded some barrels aboard. The Huron warrior, who was hiding not far from the front gate, had managed to creep undetected behind the wagons, into the settlement. Desperately trying to make his escape without being discovered, the warrior got inside one of the empty barrels and placed the lid on top. He remained absolutely still in a fetal position as the barrel, along with several others, was placed onto the waiting wagon.

Once the task had been completed, the driver drove the wagon through the front gate and down the road on its way to Boston. Sergeant Conroy caught a glimpse of the third wagon leaving Kingston as he emerged from the nearby woods. He wiped the sweat from his brow as he watched the wagon slowly fade into the distance while wishing silently that he was a passenger on that wagon taking him away from this unholy place.

---

As they rode in the carriage, Richard stared at George who was looking out the window. Richard was quite envious of his new friend's elegant attire. Then he reminded himself that he was hardly in a position to be envious of George's appearance, for Richard's tricorn hat was in good condition, although his inexpensive greatcoat was already losing some of its stiffness. His broadcloth breeches and coat always reminded him of a tradesmen whenever he caught a glimpse of himself in a mirror, and his linen, although clean, was old. He had owned one pair of civilian shoes when he had been an army officer, and he was still wearing them. There was a high polish on their silver buckles, but not even the gloss could conceal the fact that they had seen better days.

It was humiliating to be a member of the ruling class of the nation that owned these colonies and yet feel inferior to the people of the Massachusetts Bay Colony. Once again he cursed Theodore Blakeslee heartily, and he also blamed himself for having been so gullible. But the end of his journey was near; he would confront Theodore this very day, and with any luck he would clear his name and then present himself to Boston's high society and the English Crown without feeling like a pauper and a criminal.

An engraved brass plate on a heavy oak door identified the home of Theodore Blakeslee. George Dustin insisted on waiting in the carriage outside the Blakeslee residence. Richard knocked at the door and was greeted by a maid, who showed him in. She took his hat and greatcoat in an entrance hall bare of furniture, and then nodded in the direction of a drawing room, from which he could hear the sound of someone practicing scales on a small pianoforte.

He walked into the chamber: a high-ceilinged room with a few portraits on the walls, a thick woven rug on the floor, and solid but unpretentious chairs and tables.

In a far corner, at right angles to a broad hearth in which a glowing fire was burning, a pianoforte stood on four small, carved, teakwood boxes, and seated before it with her back to Richard was a young woman. She was dressed in crisp, white muslin, and a bow of the same material held her dark brown hair in place behind her neck.

She continued to pick at the keys for a moment or two, as though she did not know that someone else had come into the room. But the pretense was too much for her, and after striking a chord with more vigor than musical ability, she jumped to her feet.

"I will never learn how to play this instrument very well!" she said vehemently while turning her head.

As the young woman turned about, Richard was shocked to find himself staring at the lovely Sarah Dustin. Taken aback by seeing Sarah in Theodore's home, Richard smiled at her and began to speak, but Sarah stood still and stared at him as if he were a stranger.

# Chapter 9

**Richard smiled at Sarah** and asked her what was wrong. Sarah stared at him as if she were in a trance, and then spoke softly.

"My dear sir, do I know you? How may I help you?" she inquired.

"I have come to call upon the owner of this residence. His name is Theodore Blakeslee," replied Richard. "Are you acquainted with him?"

"Yes, I know him very well. He is indeed the owner of this lovely home, and he is my fiancé."

Shocked by Sarah's response, Richard was speechless for a moment. Then he asked Sarah once again if she knew who he was. She shrugged her shoulders to indicate that she did not know him. Richard recalled how he rescued her from the wheels of the coach the day before, and then he had dined at her home with her and her parents that same night.

Sarah began to take a walk about the room while running her fingers through her hair. In all honesty, she did not recognize Richard or remember the events that led to their first encounter. Then, without warning, Sarah placed her hand on her forehead and complained of a pain in her head before collapsing to the floor. Richard hurried to her side, picked her up in his strong arms, and carried her out of the drawing room and into the entrance hall, where he was confronted by the maid, who inquired about Sarah's condition.

"Please, give me my coat, and cover this poor young lady with it. And may I also have my hat?"

"You cannot take her from this house. My master, Mr. Blakeslee, will be very angry," said the maid.

"She is not well, and I am taking her with me. Inform Mr. Blakeslee that I shall return later to speak to him. Now, woman, please be kind enough to open the front door and let us be on our way."

As Richard went out the front door with an unconscious Sarah in his arms, someone was watching from the top of the stairs, carefully concealed in the shadows.

Once outside, Richard reached the waiting carriage, and George Dustin opened the door and assisted Richard with getting Sarah inside. They placed her on the seat and gently leaned her head against the fine upholstered backing. Then Richard shouted for the driver to leave.

As the carriage drove away, George sat next to his daughter and slowly caressed her beautiful dark brown hair while whispering softly to her that she was now safe. Then, with a troubled look upon his face, he raised his head and turned his attention to Richard, who was sitting opposite of him and Sarah.

"Thank you for rescuing my daughter yet again. I am in your debt."

"I am glad to be of assistance, but now you need to give me an explanation of what is going on. Your daughter has no memory of who I am, and her behavior was most peculiar when I encountered her. I am also shocked to learn that she is engaged to Theodore Blakeslee and spends time practicing on the pianoforte at his home. I need an explanation this instant," demanded Richard.

George apologized for the deception and told Richard that when they arrived at his home and Sarah was settled in her room, he would reveal everything to his bewildered friend. He also warned Richard that his story would be most disturbing.

---

Martha Gage was sitting in the drawing room at Huntington Hall when Mrs. Fitch entered the room.

Martha asked the housekeeper, "Where is my son?"

"Your son Thomas has taken Miss Graham to Cambridge for

a sleigh ride. They left hours ago, just after the crack of dawn, so they should be back soon. He was taking Miss Graham back to the Wentworth Mansion before he returned home. May I bring you a cup of tea?"

"Yes, that would be delightful. Thank you, Mrs. Fitch," said Martha.

For the next two hours, Martha sat in the drawing room, sipping tea and working on her needlepoint while anxiously waiting for her son's return. As she sat patiently, her mind was focused on the background of the mysterious and lovely woman with whom her son had been taken. Martha pondered over Nancy's horrific experience with the French, who had attacked and destroyed her home in Annapolis Royal. And she was curious about Nancy's family background and her interest in Thomas.

Overcome by a restless spirit, Martha could not wait a moment longer. She put down her needlepoint, rose from her chair, and sent for the carriage. She had decided to pay a call to Georgiana Wentworth in the hope of meeting up with Thomas and Nancy at the Wentworth mansion.

---

When Richard and George arrived at the Dustin home, two male servants helped to take Sarah from the carriage and brought her upstairs to her bedroom. A frantic Mabel Dustin was relieved to see her daughter. She hugged Richard while thanking him for saving her daughter from the clutches of a dangerous villain. Then she went upstairs to be with her daughter, who had started to stir and moan.

George motioned to Richard to follow him into the library, where he closed the door upon their entrance. He instructed Richard to take a seat, and then told him that the information he was about to reveal would be quite shocking and that Richard must promise to never reveal the truth about Blakeslee to any living soul, because that person would consider Richard to be a lunatic.

After Richard agreed to remain silent, George began to tell him the entire story, from when he and his family first met Theodore to the shocking events that later transpired, including an explanation for Sarah's presence at the Blakeslee residence, her strange behavior, and the unholy engagement. While an anxious Richard listened, he began to surmise that Theodore was not only a swindler who had blackened Richard's reputation and placed him in trouble with the authorities, but also an evil man who was capable of deadly intentions.

# Chapter 10

**Upon her arrival at** the Wentworth Mansion, Martha Gage was greeted by the housekeeper, who told her that Mr. and Mrs. Wentworth were not at home, but they were expected very soon. Martha informed the housekeeper that she would wait for their return and that she was hoping to see her son, who was escorting Miss Graham back to the Wentworth Mansion after their excursion to Cambridge.

The housekeeper brought Martha to the drawing room, where she was greeted by a young lady dressed in a blue silk dress and a red sash tied around her petite waist. The young girl rose from the divan in the corner of the room and politely introduced herself.

"Hello, my name is Margaret Ann Thatcher. Mr. and Mrs. Wentworth are not at home. They went to visit a neighbor but I expect them back some time soon."

For a moment, Martha stared at the lovely girl, who had dark hair and shiny blue eyes, and then remembered who she was.

"My dear Margaret Ann, it is lovely to see you. Oh my, how you have grown since the last time I saw you. You must be at least seventeen years of age."

Margaret Ann nodded with a smile and told Martha that she was correct in guessing her age. She had been ten years old when she had last visited Boston, before her guardians, Mr. and Mrs. Wentworth, sent her off to school in London. She recently finished her schooling and had been bored with London's society, so she returned to the colonies looking for excitement and possible adventure.

Martha smiled at Margaret Ann and told her that the colonies were filled with many untamed wildernesses and that life was difficult and unpredictable. She also talked about the more pleasant attractions that the booming cities of Boston, Philadelphia, and New York had to offer.

Margaret Ann remained stationary on the divan, and Martha sat in a chair adjacent to her by the hearth that had a glowing fire. For the next quarter of an hour or more, they chatted. Margaret Ann told Martha all about her years studying abroad. During their conversation, Margaret Ann picked up a bowl of candied dates and figs from a small table beside her, and offered some to Martha.

"Please, have one!" insisted Margaret Ann. "They come from Hispaniola and the Jamaica Islands in the West Indies. Mr. Wentworth's ships trade with the islanders, and the ships' captains always bring sweets back for us. There's rum in them, and they are sinfully delicious."

Martha graciously refused the girl's kind offer. She then very cautiously began to inquire about Nancy Graham. Martha pretended to show concern for Nancy by asking how she was coping after her terrible ordeal and how long she was planning to reside with the Wentworth family. Margaret Ann told an astonished Martha that Nancy was coping very well with her loss and that she intended to make Boston her new home while looking for a husband.

"I do believe Miss Graham is looking to marry a man of good fortune so she can secure her future," said Margaret Ann. "And from what I have observed in the little time of being in her company, she may have someone in mind already. If I may be honest with you, Mrs. Gage, I believe that Miss Graham is a woman who cannot be trusted. And moreover, the man she has an interest in is your son."

Upon hearing Margaret Ann's disturbing words, Martha rose from her chair, a bit agitated, and demanded that Margaret Ann further explain herself. Margaret Ann very calmly revealed to Martha that she spied on Thomas and Nancy kissing in the main entrance when Thomas had arrived to take Nancy to Cambridge. She also told Martha that on the day before, she saw Nancy concealing something in a leather box, and a few hours later the entire household was in an upheaval, searching for that same box, which Nancy had reported missing. Luckily, it was found a short time later, but Nancy had been very frantic and angry until the box was back in her possession.

"How silly it is for one to get upset over a leather box," said Margaret Ann. "In my opinion, it's quite a hideous-looking thing. But then again, it was her only treasured belonging, besides a trunk of clothing, that she has left to remind her of her home in Annapolis Royal."

Before Martha could make a reply, voices were heard from out in the hall. Then a giggling Thomas and Nancy entered the drawing room. When they saw Martha standing in the middle of the room, they both paused for a moment. Thomas went over to his mother and expressed his surprise in seeing her while giving her a peck on the cheek. Nancy gave Martha a friendly greeting as she unbuttoned a long, full cloak of white wool with a band of thick, gray fox fur on the hood, which framed her face and brought out the color in her cheeks. Beneath it she wore a plain, close-fitting dress of red wool and ankle-high red boots.

Margaret Ann excused herself and left the room but spied on them from out in the hall.

"Did you enjoy your sleigh ride and your visit to Cambridge, my dear Miss Graham? Did you also enjoy my son's company?" Martha inquired with a bit of vexation in her voice.

"I enjoyed Cambridge, the sleigh ride, and your son's company. Dear Thomas is a fine gentleman and very pleasant to be with. I'm certain that if he spent more time with the ladies of Boston's high society than with attending to his patients, he would have a large number of women from which to choose his prospective wife," said Nancy with laughter in her voice.

Martha was becoming more irritated by the moment, but she fought desperately to compose herself and informed Nancy that her son's only interest at the present time was not love for a woman, but rather his profession.

Nancy smiled at Martha while making her way across the room to the divan, and then sat down and began to unbutton her boots. Thomas went over to Nancy and offered his assistance, which she did not refuse.

Unable to remain in their presence any longer, Martha informed them that she was leaving, and she would see Thomas at home.

After putting on her overcoat, she left. On her way home, she was very upset with what she had just witnessed and was concerned about her son's friendship with this fortune-seeking, deceitful, and seductive woman.

---

At the Dustin residence, Sarah was sleeping while her mother and a maid kept a vigil by her bedside. Mabel was very concerned for her daughter's safety, and she prayed silently that the mysterious hold that Theodore Blakeslee had on her precious Sarah would be broken and that he would leave her in peace.

In the library, George told Richard that he and his family had met Theodore several months back at a ball that was hosted by a wealthy merchant, Zachary Carr, who was a partner with William Wentworth in the shipping industry. Theodore was very charming and had won the hearts of almost every person present at the ball, especially the women. Both Mabel and Sarah were taken by his elegant dress, unaffected manners, strong confidence, and mesmerizing and devilish dark eyes.

"When you stare into his eyes, you are put into a trance and become completely speechless," said George. "His behavior is very strange, filling the room with a sinister presence. And although I believed this to be true, there are others, including Mabel and Sarah, who disagreed. After our meeting at the ball, Theodore made several visits to our home, and after some time, he asked my permission to court my daughter. Against my better judgment and knowing I wouldn't have a moment of peace from my wife if I refused, I allowed him to see Sarah. In the meantime, Theodore was working closely with Zachary Carr and residing at his home. Then three months ago, one dark night, the Carr home was destroyed by a terrible fire. The servants and Theodore escaped, but Zachary Carr perished in the fire. A tomahawk was found in the front door, and the local townspeople suspected it was an attack by the Huron Indians because the Carr estate was outside the city and the colonials and British were at war with the French and their Indian allies.

"Two days after the tragedy, I went to see Theodore, who had settled into a beautiful home on Threadwell Street. To my shocking surprise, I found him in the garden with my daughter. She was sitting on a bench while Theodore was standing in front of her, holding a gold medallion in her face. When I called out to Sarah, Theodore quickly hid the medallion in his pocket, and Sarah stared at me as if I were a stranger. I frantically told Theodore to stay away from my home, and I forbid him to see my daughter. Then I quickly took hold of Sarah, and we left. As we departed, Theodore watched us while laughing wickedly."

George paused for a moment and then poured himself a glass of wine before continuing with his story. Richard did not interrupt and continued to listen in awe. After taking a few sips of wine, George went on to say that once he had returned home with Sarah, she remained in her room and did not speak to anyone. This behavior went on for several days until one afternoon, one of the servants who was attending to Sarah snapped her fingers to get the attention of another servant, and inadvertently, Sarah came out of the trance, recognized everyone, and began speaking again.

"What about Theodore Blakeslee? Did he ever return to seek out Sarah? How did they become engaged? Why did she not recognize me when I found her at his home playing the pianoforte?" interrupted an inquisitive Richard.

"About a week after the strange incident, Sarah would leave the house in the middle of the night. In the morning we would find her outside, lying on the ground. She was very cold, and her complexion was very pale. When she awoke, she had no clue what had happened. We assumed that she must have been sleepwalking. Then, two weeks later, Sarah went shopping with her mother and disappeared. We searched frantically for several hours, and then we received word in a letter written by Sarah that she was safe and residing at Theodore Blakeslee's home. Theodore then came to my home and demanded to speak with me in private. I foolishly agreed to do so, and it was then that he informed me that my beloved Sarah was under his control and they were to be married. I became angry and threatened to go to the authorities. Theodore laughed in my face and told me that if I went to the authorities, he would tell them that I was responsible for causing the fire that killed Zachary Carr. He assured me that he had enough evidence to prove my guilt, but he never elaborated on the details. He confessed that he killed Zachary Carr, because Carr had discovered he had swindled many people out of money and had framed a man by the name of Richard Hayes for the crime. I was trapped, so I went along with his evil plan. In the meantime, he allowed Sarah to be with us at certain times and also with him. When she becomes unruly, he uses that cursed medallion to put her under his spell. My Sarah is his slave.

Oh, what have I done to my precious angel? And what a coward I am!" shrieked a frustrated and frightened George.

Richard stared at George with a blank expression while taking in all that had been revealed to him. Then he walked over to George, put his hand on the sobbing man's shoulder, and promised him that he would save Sarah and deliver Theodore Blakeslee to justice one way or another. George wiped his tears and pledged his full cooperation in assisting Richard with his plan.

While the two men were speaking, a servant knocked at the door of the library and announced the arrival of a visitor, but did not say who it was. A curious Richard went to open the door, and the servant stepped aside while Theodore Blakeslee appeared in the doorway. He and Richard stared each other in the eye.

# Chapter 11

Martha returned home and retreated to the solace of the sitting room that was on the east side of Huntington Hall. She sat by the hearth and warmed her hands by the fire. As she sat staring into the flames, she began to ponder her son's friendship with Nancy Graham, which troubled her greatly. But her train of thought was interrupted by Mrs. Fitch, who announced the arrival of General Victor Kent.

The general entered the room, and Martha rose from her chair to greet her guest. Both bowed formally. Martha took an immediate liking to General Kent. He was tall, reasonably broad-shouldered, and rather handsome in a sullen way. His officer's uniform was formal and elegant, and his air indicated that he commanded respect and was very sure of himself.

Martha played the gracious hostess by inviting General Kent to take a seat, and she informed Mrs. Fitch to bring tea to her and her guest.

After the housekeeper left the room, the general complimented Martha on the elegance of her home. Then he changed the subject by inquiring about Thomas.

"How is that gifted and brilliant young surgeon? His skillful and meticulous use of a scalpel saved my son's life. I am in his debt," boasted the general.

"I thank you, sir, for your kind compliment, and I am pleased that my Thomas was able to save your son. Thomas has made the medical profession his main priority these days," replied Martha.

"I apologize for my unannounced visit, but I am here to speak to Thomas about accepting an offer to take charge of a new hospital that recently opened in Cambridge. After witnessing Thomas's surgical knowledge and compassion for his patients, especially the wounded soldiers at Fort Wilderness, I have no doubt that Thomas would be perfect for the position," the general said. "My wife, Irene, and I are contributing financially to the hospital out of gratitude for our son's life, and the desperate need for another hospital in the colonies."

"I know that my son would be honored by your offer, dear general. I have always been proud and supportive of his accomplishments, particularly his desire to practice medicine," said Martha a bit deceivingly. "He is visiting a friend, but I expect him to return very soon. In the meantime, please join me in a cup of tea and polite conversation."

"My dear lady, it would be my pleasure to visit with you while I wait for your son's return home," replied a smiling General Kent.

---

At the Dustin residence, Theodore went into the library and Richard closed the door behind them and then turned his attention to Theodore. Theodore made his way to a nervous George, who was shaking in his boots. Theodore was dressed in a brocade suit and a dark greatcoat that made his appearance very foreboding.

"Are you telling each other tales about me? Gentlemen, let me warn the both of you that I can destroy you with the blink of my eye," laughed a wicked Theodore. "I am the only witness who can clear Richard's name and prevent him from going to jail. And my foolish George, I hold your precious and beautiful daughter's fate in my hands, as well as your own."

Richard defiantly walked up to Theodore and stared directly into his dark, malevolent eyes and then boldly spoke.

"You are going to clear my name by informing the governor and the authorities about your crimes of stealing money from my associates and me, and then you will confess to the murder of Zachary Carr and release Mr. Dustin from your bastardly grip of blackmail. And finally, you will relinquish your mysterious spell on sweet Sarah Dustin. We shall escort you to the constable's office this very day," replied a brave and determined Richard as he reached for Theodore's left arm.

"You are both insolent and pathetic fools who shall now meet my wrath," shrieked a crazed Theodore with evil in his eyes.

As Richard moved forward in an attempt to subdue his fiendish adversary, Theodore removed some pellets from his coat pocket and tossed them into the fireplace, causing the room to become filled with heavy smoke. The smoke caused Richard and George to cough profusely and make it impossible to see their hands in front of them. These horrible and blinding conditions made it convenient for Theodore to escape.

# Chapter 12

Richard and George found their way out of the library and into the hallway. Both men were perspiring heavily, and their clothing smelled of the hearth. George instructed two of the servants to open the windows and let winter's cold air and chilly wind into the room as a means to dispense with the smoke. Once the burning sensation from the smoke had ceased from his eyes, Richard hurried upstairs to Sarah's bedroom, where he found her asleep in bed and Mabel sitting in a chair not far from her daughter's bedside, reading the Bible. Mabel raised her head and was startled by Richard's appearance.

"Is everything all right? You look very troubled. Has that horrible Theodore Blakeslee tried to enter this home in an attempt to take my beloved Sarah?" asked an agitated Mabel.

"Do not worry, Mrs. Dustin. Your husband and I have managed to deal with him. Sarah is safe, and I promise you that she shall remain that way."

Then Richard quietly closed the door behind him and went downstairs. He found George sitting in a chair in the entrance hall, drinking a glass of water with his manservant at his side. Richard asked George if the manservant could accompany him outside to search the grounds to make certain that Theodore had left the property. George gave his permission and stayed behind to keep watch over Sarah. Richard removed a pistol from under his jacket as he and the manservant went outside. Unbeknownst to them, Theodore was lurking about in the nearby distance.

---

When Thomas returned to Huntington Hall, he was quite surprise to find his mother and General Kent conversing and drinking tea in the sitting room. They were engaged in cheerful conversation that apparently had put a smile on Martha's face. Thomas went up to his mother and gently kissed her on the cheek. General Kent rose to his feet and shook hands with Thomas.

"My dear son, where have you been?" asked Martha. "I expected your return much sooner. While you were out, General Kent came to see you, and he has graced me with his delightful company and told me stories about serving in His Majesty's glorious army. I am very impressed."

"General Kent, I am surprised to see you. Is everything all right with your son, Cooper?" asked Thomas.

"Yes, everything is fine. Cooper is recovering nicely from his wounds, all thanks to you. I came to Huntington Hall to speak with you about a business proposition that I believe shall entice you greatly," replied the general.

Before Thomas could say another word, Martha politely excused herself, allowing her son and the general to talk privately. When she went into the hallway, she found a maid scrubbing the floor. When she asked the young woman why she was scrubbing the floor, the servant told her she was cleaning the mud and wet snow that Thomas and his companion, Miss Graham, had brought into the house on their shoes.

"Miss Graham was here in this house?" inquired a vexed Martha.

"Yes, she came inside for a few minutes, and then she departed. I overheard her tell your son that she had to pay a call to Mr. and Mrs. Dustin," answered the maid.

Martha was not pleased to learn that Nancy Graham had come to Huntington Hall. And she was even more curious to know Nancy's reason for calling on the Dustins. She left the young maid to finish her task and quietly tiptoed down the hallway, returning to the sitting room, where she stood outside the doorway, eavesdropping on the conversation between Thomas and General Kent.

---

Back at the Dustin residence, Richard and George's manservant searched the grounds diligently, but found no trace of Theodore Blakeslee. After some time had passed, Richard told the servant to return to the house and said he would return momentarily.

After the servant had left, Richard walked to the stables. A chilly, winter wind hissed at his face as he looked at the barren trees and the light snow on the bushes. All was silent except for the sound of his footsteps walking on the fallen leaves that lined the ground under the muddy and lightly snow-covered ground.

Suddenly, he stopped for a moment due to a strange feeling that someone was behind him. With his pistol in hand, he slowly turned around, and, to his surprise, he saw Nancy Graham standing before him.

# Chapter 13

Although he was taken aback by Nancy's presence on the grounds of the Dustin residence, Richard was glad to see her. Nancy was certainly no less lovely than the first time they had met. Her hair, softly waved at her temples and over her forehead, was a perfect frame for her blushing face. Her overcoat was unbuttoned, exposing her gown that was pale yellow silk with a wide, square neck, edged with black velvet, and a black velvet ribbon binding her bodice close to her from beneath her chest to her waist. Her gently waving full skirt brushed the tips of her matching yellow silk shoes. All this somehow enhanced her femininity despite the fact that she was not the fragile type.

Nancy appeared to be unaware of the effect she was creating, and her simplicity and naturalness removed any suspicion from Richard's mind that she might be deliberately flirting with him. The provocative quality that had attracted him to her from the first was still present, and her appeal and sudden appearance was distracting him from his search for Theodore.

"My dear Nancy, what are you doing here? I am searching these grounds for a dangerous man. It is not safe for you to be wandering about alone," said a concerned Richard.

Nancy smiled but did not respond while her fingers opened her overcoat completely, and then she placed her hands on her bosom. On sudden impulse, Richard reached out and put his hand over hers. She started to draw away from him, but something stopped her, and she allowed him to clasp her hand. The feeling of mutual sympathy and understanding that attracted them to each other became stronger, more insistent, causing Richard to drop his pistol. He reached for her, but Nancy struggled as he took her in his arms.

"No," she murmured. "Please, I'm not that sort of person."

"I didn't think you were," he replied. "I swear to you that I'll never do anything to hurt you."

With one arm, he encircled her waist, and with his other hand at the small part of her back, he drew her gently to him. She trembled for an instant, and then she sighed and yielded to him. Nancy lifted her face, and they looked full into each other's eyes before Richard kissed her. The kiss was quiet at first, curiously sweet and tender, as though they had long been lovers. But gradually their passion mounted, and Richard became increasingly aware of Nancy's vibrant warmth. His hold tightened as she curled her arms around his neck, and they pressed together, unmindful of anything but each other and the emotions that all but overwhelmed them.

Ahead, in a clearing devoid of trees, Richard's nemesis, Theodore, was watching with a demonic satisfaction. In his mind, Nancy had been the most convenient distraction preventing Richard from hunting him down like an animal. Theodore mounted his horse and then rode into the distance.

---

At the Wentworth Mansion, Margaret Ann. after some solitary time in her room, put on a blue overcoat and went outside for a breath of fresh air. The cool crisp March wind felt refreshing against her cheeks. She walked down to the stables, and upon her entrance, she found two of the horses eating hay that was piled neatly in a corner of the stall. As she stood for a moment and glanced at the two beasts, she giggled at the way they chewed their food. Then her amusement was interrupted by a strange rustling sound coming from the stall at the far end of the stables.

Margaret Ann picked up a pitch fork and slowly made her way toward the place where the sound was coming from. Upon reaching her destination, she stood erect with the pitch fork held firmly in her hands while bravely confronting a young Indian warrior. The young warrior stood tall and proud, and did not flinch while his dark brown eyes stared intensely at the young, lovely woman.

Margaret Ann was captivated by the warrior's muscular arms and chest, and his long, luscious black hair that hung below his broad shoulders. His attire, consisting of a breechcloth from the waist down and moccasins on his feet, added to his attractive yet rough appearance. After momentarily relinquishing her sensual desires, she mustered up the courage to speak.

"Who are you? And what are you doing hiding in my uncle's stables? This is a shelter for the animals, not intruders," she replied in a flustered and nervous tone. "Do you speak English?"

"My name is Black Crow. I am a Huron warrior. My mother was a Huron, and my father was a French fur trapper. My father taught me how to speak English and French, while my mother taught me the tongue of the Huron. When I was ten years old, my parents were killed by an enemy tribe, but I survived and went to live with my grandfather, Chief Little Turtle and his tribe," he explained.

"I am sorry about your parents, but what brings you here? Are you hiding from someone, like the British soldiers, or looking to steal my uncle's horses?" inquired a curious Margaret Ann.

"My fellow Huron warriors were killed by the militia during an attack on a fortress north of this place. I am the only survivor. I do not mean you any harm."

Black Crow's good looks and deep voice put Margaret Ann's fears to rest, but she did not dispense of the pitch fork.

Realizing that the young woman before him seemed enticed by his presence, Black Crow continued to speak to her, explaining that he had escaped from the fortress by carefully concealing himself in a barrel that was transported by wagon to the city, and that along the ride, he got out of the barrel, went into the woods, and eventually reached the stables, where he sought shelter. Margaret Ann was intrigued by his story and admired his bravery and tenacity. As they continued to talk, she revealed her name, and they became slowly more acquainted with one another. After some time, she became a bit more trusting and put down the pitch fork as she boldly approached Black Crow.

Then, to Black Crow's astonishment, she wrapped her arms around his waist and rested her head on his muscular chest, just below his chin. She closed her eyes for a moment and sighed. A startled Black

Crow remained still and then placed his arms gently around Margaret Ann's waist, holding her against his half-naked body. Although they were strangers meeting for the first time, their mutual attraction and affection for each other was strong and undeniable.

When Margaret Ann finally released her arms from around Black Crow's waist, she raised her head and stared aimlessly into his dark brown eyes while he stared into her majestic blue eyes. When they finished staring at each other, she told him to remain in the stables and wait for her while she went to the main house to get some food.

"I will return shortly with food and drink. Please stay out of sight. I will not tell a living soul that you are here," she said as she hurried out of the stables, closing the door behind her.

Black Crow sat down on a pile of hay and waited patiently for her return. On her way up to the main house, she continued to feel the strong and warm embrace of Black Crow's arms around her and his muscular and physically attractive body pressed up against her. Although Black Crow was a savage and heathen from the wilderness, she sensed that he had tender emotions and a loving heart. His magnificent upper torso reminded her of Michelangelo's sculpture of David. Black Crow was certainly a prize that Margaret Ann was determined to keep, but she knew that her desire to be with him would have serious consequences.

# Chapter 14

After a solitary and expensive supper at the Fairview Inn, Richard donned a clean shirt, buckled on his sword, and set out for the Wentworth Mansion to see Nancy. He could not get her off his mind or forget the passionate kiss they shared. He also did not accept her explanation of why she had come to call upon Mr. and Mrs. Dustin while he was pursuing the dastardly Theodore on the Dustin estate. His curiosity demanded an honest and logical reason, and he could not sleep a wink until he got one.

Richard had traveled a great distance on little more than hope to find and confront the swindler who had wronged him and his associates while bringing scandal and the threat of imprisonment upon him. But now, Theodore, by his recent actions and disturbing obsession with an innocent Sarah Dustin, was not only a swindler but a dangerous man who had to be stopped. Richard's money would soon evaporate, so he knew he was on borrowed time to clear his name. Therefore, he assumed an air of confidence and determination to find Theodore and bring him to justice.

When he had arrived at the Wentworth Mansion, a manservant in a maroon silk outfit answered the door and asked Richard the purpose for his visit while blocking the doorframe. Richard told the servant that he had come to see Nancy Graham, Mr. and Mrs. Wentworth's house guest. As he spoke, they were suddenly interrupted by a faintly husky feminine voice from within.

"Let the gentleman come in. I shall attend to him."

The door swung open, and an attractive older woman stood in the hallway beneath a cut-glass chandelier ablaze with the finest French tapers. She was tiny but perfectly formed, and her clinging gown of pale ivory satin, which revealed as much as it concealed of her considerable charms, was a tribute both to the skill of her dressmaker and to her own bone structure. Her skin was very white and contrasted strongly with her dark hair, which she wore shoulder-length but brushed back like a man's. Her long pendant diamond earrings sparkled, and she was smiling in welcome as Richard entered and bowed to her.

"Welcome to my brother and sister-in-law's home—Mr. and Mrs. Wentworth," she said gently, and held out a cool hand on which a large emerald ring was prominent.

Richard, totally unprepared for a greeting by such an elegant and attractive creature, especially an older one, was momentarily speechless.

"I am Irene Wentworth Kent," she continued. "My maiden name was Wentworth before I married an English general named Victor Kent from Bath. I am visiting my husband and son, who will be returning shortly from Fort Wilderness. In the meantime, I am residing here at my brother's lovely home as a guest and grateful lodger. Won't you come in and please follow me?" she exclaimed as she moved down a corridor while elegantly and gingerly switching the bustle and train of her gown.

As Richard followed her, he was conscious of the scent of her perfume, which was stronger than that worn by ladies in England, but seemed to suit her.

The small drawing room into which she took him was furnished with elaborate furniture. The backs, legs, and arms of chairs were ornately carved, as were the edges of tables. There were many cushions everywhere, most of them embroidered in gold and silver. A large and intricately woven tapestry dominated one wall, and the other walls were lined with portraits. On the mantel above a fireplace stood a clock of brilliant cloisonné enamel and a marble statuette of a woman and child. The decorations in the room were overwhelming to Richard, and he marveled at how the privileged class lived so elegantly and extravagantly while commoners lived in poverty and misery, struggling each day to survive.

For a moment, Irene busied herself with a decanter, and then came to Richard with two crystal glasses in her hands. She stood close to him for a moment while gracefully pouring wine into his glass. Then she did the same with her glass before proposing a strange toast.

"A drop of sack is cheering on a cold night," she said.

While Irene and Richard sipped their wine politely and smiled at each other, their solitude was interrupted by Nancy Graham's entrance into the room. Nancy was dressed in a provocative gown, and the low cut of the dress made Richard feel uncomfortable as she stood in front of him. The expression in her eyes and the way she held herself caused him to have sexual intentions that he found difficult to suppress.

"Richard, this is a wonderful and unexpected surprise. Were you waiting long for me?" asked Nancy as she put her hands up to her bosoms and smiled seductively.

Irene instantly felt the sexual tension that was mounting between Nancy and Richard, so she politely excused herself. Before she departed, she told Richard that it was a delight to have met him, and that she hoped to see him again.

---

After Irene left the drawing room, she went upstairs to her quarters. She closed the bedroom door, and, feeling a bit restless, she took a turn about the room. She went over to the window, and as she peered through the glass, she caught a glimpse of what appeared to be someone carrying a lantern and walking down to the stables. Her curiosity got the better of her, so she decided to take a walk down to the stables to seek out this individual and find out what was going on.

---

In the drawing room, Richard had finished his wine and walked over to Nancy, who was sitting quite comfortably on a divan, nestled in between several cushions. Richard knelt down before Nancy to afford eye contact with her. Then, in a calm voice, he asked her the real reason for her presence at the Dustin estate earlier in the day. Nancy began to run her fingers through her hair while pushing her bosoms in Richard's direction.

"I told you that I had heard that Sarah Dustin was not feeling well, so I paid a call to inquire about her health and to lend my support to the family," Nancy replied very cunningly.

"I do not believe you, because you barely know Sarah Dustin and her family. Why would the health of someone you hardly know concern you? I want the truth, and do not try to distract me by flaunting yourself like a Jezebel."

"Do not deny your feelings for me or what we had shared for that brief time just hours ago," said Nancy. "Let us not argue but concentrate on our genuine and passionate desires for one another. Please embrace me and kiss me like you did before."

Richard tried desperately to stay focused on the real reason for his visit, but Nancy's flamboyance and seductive wiles conquered him. He quickly gave into his feelings and firmly took hold of Nancy and pressed his lips against hers. They passionately kissed while becoming one with one another. As Nancy and Richard busied themselves, satisfying their unquenchable sexual desire, they were unaware that Theodore Blakeslee was watching them from outside the terrace doors with a devilish satisfaction.

# Chapter 15

**When Margaret Ann returned** to the stables, she found Black Crow waiting for her return. She hurried to him and placed before him a sack filled with various types of food. He thanked her for her kindness and began to eat ravenously, because it had been nearly two days since his last meal. Margaret Ann excused his poor manners and ate a piece of fruit daintily while sitting on the ground. As she watched Black Crow eat, she studied him closely and was enthralled by his good looks. She wished that some of the young gentlemen of the colonies and London were as magnificently attractive.

After Black Crow had finished his meal, he asked his gracious hostess if he could spend the night in the stables, and said that he would leave just before dawn. A disappointed Margaret Ann quickly rose to her feet and told Black Crow that she would not allow him to leave and return to the wilderness. She begged him to stay and promised him that she would devise a plan for them to become better acquainted without anyone's interference. Black Crow stared at the young, beautiful, and somewhat naïve Margaret Ann with awe, but he knew that he and she could not be companions because they were from different walks of life, and the rules of society would forbid a relationship between them.

"We can never be together because you are a well-bred English lady, and I am from the wilderness, and I belong to a tribe that is the enemy of your people. Also, your family would never allow us to see each other, let alone give us their blessing for a future together. It is something that cannot ever be, so we must accept reality right here and now," said an adamant Black Crow.

"I will not let you go. I have no family. I have been raised by Mr. and Mrs. Wentworth, who have been so kind and generous to me these seventeen years. Out of respect and gratitude, I call them my aunt and uncle," explained Margaret Ann. "I am not tempted by the young men of my society and social class, or any man for that matter, but you have captivated me from the first moment I saw you. Please, I beg of you, give us a chance. Friendship and love will conquer all, including the disdainful prejudices of the civilized world," she pleaded.

"It will not work. For the last time, we cannot be together, and I have nothing more to say on the matter. I thank you for the food and hospitality, but now I will bid you farewell," Black Crow responded as he rose to his feet and began to walk to the door of the stables.

"No. You cannot leave me," cried Margaret Ann. "I will not let you go."

In a desperate attempt to stop Black Crow, Margaret Ann grabbed hold of his left leg and tried to pull him to his knees. But his strength was no match for her. She lost her grip, and he continued on his way. She tenaciously hurried after him and succeeded in wrapping her arms around him, begging him not to go. Lacking the courage to leave, Black Crow turned around and took Margaret Ann into his muscular arms. As she surrendered into his arms, they stared into each other's eyes and then slowly locked lips, exchanging a passionate kiss. Both felt a powerful connection that pleased them very much.

Suddenly, to their dismay, the door to the stables opened. Standing in their way was Irene Kent. With one hand she held a lantern. The other hand covered her mouth as she tried not to scream from the shock of her discovery.

---

Back in the drawing room of the main house, Richard abruptly broke free from Nancy while struggling desperately to resist her physical appeal. He wanted so much to give into his desire, yet he knew that if he did, he would be committing himself to far more than a romantic liaison with an attractive young woman who was deliberately hiding something from him.

"I will not let you distract me. I came here this evening to see you and learn the truth of why you were at the Dustin estate. I want an answer this instant," he demanded.

A cunning Nancy slowly smiled at him and looked him up and down. She changed the subject by attempting to entice him with a compliment.

"Have you ever caught a glimpse of yourself in a mirror? There are not many men in Boston who can wear a uniform with such distinct confidence. I've seen them all, and I know."

Richard cynically gazed down at her, pleased by her flattery. He knew he would enjoy making love to her, and he wondered whether he could play her game without losing sight of his ultimate objectives.

Within seconds, he came to his senses and was determined to resist the tempting and attractive creature before him.

Nancy remained positioned on the divan, slowly wetting her lips. Richard turned away from her as he looked in the direction of the terrace doors, where he saw Theodore Blakeslee spying on them.

A strong rush of anger filled his body as he ran to the terrace doors. He flung the doors open with great force. As Theodore tried to make his escape, he tripped and fell to the ground. Within seconds, Richard was upon him. He grabbed Theodore by his neck and lifted him to his feet. Then, looking Theodore in the face, Richard punched him in the stomach, causing Theodore to slouch in pain.

Nancy witnessed the punch, and she gave out a scream that alerted a handful of servants and William and Georgiana Wentworth, who had just returned home.

Richard took a strong hold of Theodore and escorted him forcefully inside, where William Wentworth demanded an explanation for what had transpired between the two men. Theodore cowardly spoke and blamed Richard for attacking him, but Richard explained venomously Theodore's wrongdoings against him, his associates, and the Dustin family, including poor Sarah Dustin.

After hearing Richard's shocking story, William Wentworth instructed one of his servants to get the constable. He then told Richard that he had his permission to detain Theodore at his home until the authorities arrived. Richard put Theodore in a chair and told him not to move while he watched over him with a pistol in hand.

William, Georgiana, and the servants exited the room, leaving

Richard, Theodore, and Nancy behind. Nancy was nervous, and when she looked up at Richard, she knew that he was on to her. She made another attempt to smile at him, but she realized it was a futile gesture, and she sighed deeply. Theodore gave her the evil eye, which made chills run down her spine.

As Richard was about to confront Nancy in Theodore's presence, Georgiana entered the room, insisting that Nancy follow her, as Georgiana told her it was inappropriate for her to remain with the two men, particularly since one was accused of criminal acts.

As Nancy slowly took her leave, Richard grabbed her arm.

"I am not finished with you. We will talk very soon, and you will tell me and the authorities the truth. For your sake, I hope and pray that you are not in anyway connected to this deceitful and dangerous man," he uttered angrily.

Nancy did not speak a word. Richard released his grip, and she left the room. As she was walking out of the room, Richard wondered how anyone so beautiful could be so calculatingly deceitful. At least he had Theodore in his grasp, and perhaps now justice would be served. Theodore stared at Richard with a contemptuous glare and a wicked smirk on his face.

"I warned you not to meddle in my affairs," said Theodore, clenching his fists with vengeance. "You may feel that you have won by capturing me and delivering me to the authorities, but I promise you that your victory will be very short-lived. Before I am through with you, you will be sorry that you were ever born."

# Chapter 16

At Huntington Hall, Thomas was standing by the hearth, staring into the flames of the warm fire. He was pondering General Kent's offer to practice his surgical skills at a hospital in Cambridge. Although Thomas was devoted to his profession, he was starting to question whether he wanted to continue working with the sick and wounded after the horrific sights of death and suffering he had witnessed at Fort Wilderness. As he continued to stare into the flames, he began to see Nancy's face, which brought a sense of comfort to him. He started to smile while imaging Nancy and him dancing at a ball, swirling about the room without a care in the world.

"Are you deep in thought about General Kent's generous offer?" inquired a curious Martha as she entered the drawing room.

Thomas was a bit irritated by his mother's interruption. He knew that she would be relentless until he made a decision. He was reluctant to speak to his mother about his conversation with General Kent. Martha smiled at her son and invited him to sit with her, but Thomas informed his mother that he was tired and wanted to turn in early. He took a glass of sherry and then said good night as he made his way upstairs to his bedroom.

A disappointed Martha began to suspect that Thomas was making an excuse to avoid her. She had longed for the day when her son would marry a young aristocratic woman who would make him happy and give him children. But now she feared that he had doubts about his future plans to remain a surgeon and settle down, unless, of course, his choice was Nancy Graham.

Martha decided to give Thomas a few days to make his decision without berating him. In the meantime, she would occupy her time by getting better acquainted with Nancy and finding out what her intentions were concerning her son.

---

Nearly an hour had passed before the authorities reached the Wentworth Mansion. When they finally arrived, Theodore sat in silence while Richard gave his account of Theodore's crimes. When the constable asked Theodore to speak in his defense, Theodore calmly stared at the officer and protested that the allegations were false. He then demanded that he be released unless Richard could produce solid evidence to prove his guilt. Richard informed the constable that he had witnesses ready to testify against the accused.

After scratching his gray-haired wig, the constable decided to take Theodore into custody and ordered Richard to bring the witnesses to the governor's office in the morning, where the matter would be investigated.

As the constable and his men were escorting Theodore out of the house, Theodore stared at Richard as unpleasant thoughts filled his mind. It was at that moment that Richard realized Theodore was quite capable of inflicting harm on other human beings, and his concern focused now on his suspicion about Nancy's involvement with Theodore.

"If you're wise, you won't stir up trouble, and you'll let us settle our differences privately. This isn't England, where everyone behaves according to conventions that have been established over hundreds of years," said Theodore in a brittle tone.

"Are you threatening me now? The truth shall prevail, and you will be brought to justice," uttered an undefeated Richard.

As Theodore walked away, he was determined to have the last word. Theodore did not want the constable to hear him so he whispered to Richard.

"Boston isn't far from the wilderness, you know. And in the wilderness, there are no rules," he said, leaving those words to fester in Richard's mind.

At the stables, Irene took a moment to compose her thoughts after finding Margaret Ann in the arms of the Huron warrior. Then she calmly demanded an explanation. Margaret Ann greeted Irene and told her that she had nothing to fear from Black Crow. Irene was very intrigued about what was taking place, and she was captivated by Black Crow's magnificent physical appearance. She stared at his muscular arms and chest while she listened to Margaret Ann.

"My dear and favorite Aunt Irene, I want to introduce Black Crow to you. He is a Huron warrior, but he means us no harm. He escaped from a massacre and was seeking a place to rest in the stable. He is unlike the other savages as he is kind and speaks very good English," she said while determined to win her aunt's approval of Black Crow. "His parents, a Frenchman and a Huron squaw, died when he was young, and he lived with his grandfather, a Huron chief. There is something very special about him. He is most pleasing to me in comparison to the young Englishmen of my acquaintance."

"My dear Margaret Ann, there is no way that you can consider having a friendship with him, let alone a courtship. It is unacceptable by the rules and customs of our society. I agree with you that he is a fine specimen of the male race, but he is an uncivilized savage who is an ally of the French. He needs to leave immediately, and you need to never think or speak of him again," said an adamant Irene. "It is the way things must be."

Vexed by her aunt's words, Margaret Ann refused to take her advice. She grabbed hold of Black Crow and begged him to take her with him, but he disappointed her by agreeing with Irene. He told Margaret Ann that they could not be together and must part company that same night. Margaret Ann began to rant like a spoiled child. Irene raised her voice and demanded that her niece put an end to her uncouth behavior. But Margaret Ann ignored her aunt and continued to rant.

Suddenly, a loud voice was heard from outside the stables. It was William Wentworth calling for Margaret Ann.

"Please, Aunt Irene, do not give Black Crow away. I beg of you, do not reveal his presence to Uncle William. Hurry, Black Crow, hide this instant."

William made his way to the stables, and upon his arrival, he found that the door was closed. He opened it, walked inside, and he found Irene to be the only one present. She looked at her brother and gave him a jovial greeting. When he inquired about Margaret Ann, she fibbed by telling him that his niece was asleep in her bed. When he asked Irene why she was at the stables, she lied again, saying that she had felt restless and decided to take a walk to see the horses.

As Irene and William were speaking, Margaret Ann was snuggled in Black Crow's arms, only a few feet away in the next stall.

# Chapter 17

Governor Jonathon Fenton, the king's viceroy for Massachusetts, was a rare executive who enjoyed both the support of the colony and the confidence of King George III's ministers in London. His wisdom and fairness made him unique among the representatives of the Crown in the colonies, and under his guidance, the colony of Massachusetts flourished as it had once before under the leadership of his predecessor, Grant Marshall. Those laws made by a distant Parliament, which tended to discriminate against the colonies or stifle or limit their development, were ignored by Governor Fenton, who nevertheless was careful to instill in his subjects a respect for the king and the mother country.

The governor encouraged the growth of trade; made it easy for immigrants to establish titles to lands on the frontier, which was constantly moving westward; and believed in uniting the colonies in time of war. He had long expressed the opinion that a continuing series of wars between England and France were inevitable and that the struggle would continue until one or the other was driven from the North American continent. He had hoped that England would be victorious and that the colonies would continue to prosper. When war had broken out with France seven years earlier, Fenton was not surprised, but he was currently pleased that a peace treaty was about to be signed and the English were victorious.

Early the next morning Governor Fenton, a tall, heavy-set figure dressed in black broadcloth and a modest-looking wig upon his head, was at the office where he conducted the affairs of Massachusetts.

He was sitting at a large table of polished oak on which papers were placed in neat piles, and a painting of the king was the only decoration on the wall. An assistant entered the room and handed Fenton a legal document concerning the case against Theodore Blakeslee. The governor read the document and was very upset when he read the part about Theodore's threats against George Dustin and his daughter. The Dustins were friends of the governor and he considered them to be loyal subjects of the Crown.

He was greatly disturbed by the case, and he ordered his assistant to send word to the constable to bring the accused and all those involved to his office within the hour. After the assistant left, Fenton wrote a message on a piece of parchment and placed it inside his desk. Then he stared out the window while listening to the church bells of Christ Church ringing from down the street.

---

At breakfast, William and Georgiana were talking about the arrest of Theodore Blakeslee and were very disturbed about the accusations lodged against him. They had regarded him as a respected and proper gentleman who had nicely settled into Boston society.

Irene listened politely, but she was preoccupied thinking about Margaret Ann and her Indian friend. She could not get her niece's behavior and fixation with Black Crow out of her mind. She also knew that her niece could be a very stubborn and determined young woman. At that moment, Irene was wishing that Margaret Ann had fallen in love with a young man from one of Boston's prominent families; even the son of a commoner would not be as scandalous as a savage from the frontier.

After they had finished their meal, William went to the docks to check on his ships that had returned the night before from the islands, and Georgiana retired to the library to catch up on her invitations for the ball.

Irene hurried upstairs to Margaret Ann's bedroom and frantically knocked at the door. She was relieved when her niece opened the door and, with a pleasant smile, invited her in. Margaret Ann sat down at the dressing table and began to brush her hair while making polite conversation with Irene, who instantly changed the subject by inquiring about Black Crow.

"We missed you at breakfast. One of the servants informed us that you decided to sleep in."

"Yes, my dear aunt, I was exhausted from being up late last night, so I did not awake from my warm and comfortable bed until a short time ago. It is good to see you, but will you please excuse me while I finish dressing?"

"When you have finished dressing, we need to have a serious conversation. Please, come to my room so we may speak in private. Before I leave, I must ask you, where is Black Crow?"

Before Margaret Ann could reply, a noise was heard from the adjoining room. Irene went quickly to investigate while an agitated Margaret Ann hurried after her. When she entered the room, Irene's eyes opened wide as she gazed upon a naked Black Crow washing his face in a basin on a table by the bed. Startled and embarrassed by Irene's abrupt intrusion, he jumped into the bed, covering himself with a quilt.

"Good heavens. What is going on in this place? My dear Margaret Ann, I do believe you have gone too far this time. There must be an end to this outlandish friendship or attachment or whatever you may wish to call it, this instant," replied a flustered Irene as she tried to find composure. "What if someone like my brother or his wife were to stumble upon Black Crow, particularly in his present condition? Do you realize what the consequence would be?"

Margaret Ann was unaffected by Irene's comments and remained quite calm during her aunt's brief outburst from worry and embarrassment. She told Irene that after everyone had gone to sleep and the household was very quiet, she sneaked Black Crow into the house and he slept in the adjoining room as she did not want the stable hands to find him when they came to work in the early morning.

"Black Crow is a gentleman and treats me like a lady," said a very delighted Margaret Ann. "As a matter of fact, he has more manners than many of these Englishmen, and I bet he could teach them a thing or two about the proper way to treat a young lady."

Irene shook her head in astonishment while realizing that her niece was truly in awe over Black Crow and that this was a very bad thing. She instructed Margaret Ann to return to her room and finish dressing, and she told Black Crow to return to his task at hand once they had left the room. Then she closed the door of the adjoining room and pleaded with her niece and her Indian companion to remain quiet in the room with the door locked until her return.

As Irene was making her way downstairs, a servant approached her and said there was a gentleman by the name of Lord Amherst waiting to see her in the drawing room. Irene was very well acquainted with her guest but surprised and curious about his visit. As Irene and the servant descended the staircase, Nancy emerged from the shadows upstairs, tiptoed to Margaret Ann's room, and leaned up against the door with a listening ear.

---

At the governor's office, a confident Richard stood tall in the only civilian outfit that he had owned, which he had brought from London to the colonies. He told his story about Theodore stealing money from him and his associates, and Theodore's threats and unlawful acts against George Dustin and his family. He was careful not to speak of the murder of Zachary Carr, because there was no evidence to support George's innocence and because Richard was uncertain about the proof that Theodore had claimed to possess that implicated George in the crime. Richard was determined to let nothing dissuade him or prevent him from recovering his money, clearing his name, and delivering Theodore to justice. After Richard had finished speaking, he took his place alongside George Dustin. Mabel was not present as she had remained at home with Sarah, who was not well enough to attend the hearing. Theodore sat in silence, staring at Richard venomously.

Then it was George's turn to speak. He was a bit shaky because he was afraid to face Theodore. Yet he held himself together while he gave his account of Theodore's obsession and inappropriate control over his daughter, and his threat against the family.

Governor Fenton as well as the constable listened intently, and when George had finished speaking, all those present in the room were shocked and puzzled by what they had heard. After a few moments of silence, Governor Fenton turned to Theodore and gave him permission to speak.

A crafty Theodore rose slowly from his wooden chair, looked at the governor, and then turned to stare at Richard and George. Then he coughed, and placed his hand over his heart, and faced the governor again before speaking.

"Milord Governor Fenton, I am a loyal subject of the Crown and a hard-working colonist who has made a home in this prosperous city of Boston. I obey all the laws while respecting and showing Christian charity toward those less fortunate than myself. I do not owe any money to Major Hayes, and I resent the fact that he has blamed me for his failed investments. As far as my relationship with the beautiful daughter of George Dustin, it is of mutual consent; and not too long ago, Mr. Dustin gave his consent and blessing for us to be married. In all honesty, I do not know why these outrageous and unfounded tales are being spoken about me, and why we are wasting your precious time with all this nonsense?"

Furious by Theodore's pitiful and untruthful statement, Richard sprang from his chair like a mountain cat and lunged at Theodore, calling him a liar and a thief.

"Confess your crimes this very instant," shouted an angry Richard.

It took the constable and two other officers to get Richard away from Theodore. Governor Fenton banged his gavel fiercely on the desk while calling for the restoration of order. After Richard was restrained by the constable and his men, Theodore stood erect while calmly facing those in the room. Then his arms began to shake, followed by his legs, and his head started to jerk from side to side. Finally, he gave out a loud cry before collapsing. Richard as well as the others stood in shock as they stared at Theodore lying very still on the cold wooden floor.

# Chapter 18

When she entered the drawing room, Irene found a well-dressed and distinguished Lord Jeffrey Amherst standing by the fireplace, patiently waiting for her. They both bowed formally to one another, and then Irene invited him to sit with her.

"Lord Jeffrey, what an unexpected but pleasant surprise! How are you? It is wonderful news that the war has ended and we shall finally be rid of the French."

"I am very well, thank you. And yes, it is very good news that the war is over and the colonists can live in peace. I need a respite from the dreadful roar of cannons and gunfire, and the horrific sight of the wounded and the dead," he replied solemnly. "I am a messenger bringing you a letter that General James Wolfe had entrusted me to deliver to you. It was his final wish before he closed his eyes forever. The good general is dead, and so is his long-time adversary, the Marquis de Montcalm."

Irene expressed her sympathy concerning General Wolfe's demise. She began to reminisce with Lord Jeffrey about the times when they all attended the grand gatherings at St. James' Palace. Then Lord Jeffrey inquired about Margaret Ann, the mischievous ten-year-old, who had enjoyed playing tricks on him when he came to visit. He was only seven years her senior, and he had a fondness for her. Irene noticed that when Lord Jeffrey spoke of her niece, he was smiling broadly.

Following their conversation, Lord Jeffrey took a letter from his coat pocket and handed it to Irene. He told her that the general wanted her to have the letter and to protect the secret that was concealed inside it. Irene stared at him for a few moments with an intrigued and puzzled look, and then she placed the letter on a nearby table. She insisted that Lord Jeffrey stay for tea, but he turned down her gracious offer and took his leave.

Once he was gone, Irene unsealed the letter and began to read it.

---

The constable and his officers managed to bring an unconscious Theodore to the jail across the street. Governor Fenton asked his assistant to send for a doctor. Due to the unforeseen circumstances, the governor had no choice but to postpone the hearing. He ordered both Richard and George to keep their distance from Theodore.

George offered Richard a carriage ride back to the Fairview Inn. Richard declined and told his friend that he preferred to walk back to the inn, as he felt that the exercise and fresh air would help to clear his mind.

As Richard walked the streets, he was convinced that Theodore had cleverly orchestrated this little charade in an effort to delay facing justice for his crimes. A knot of hard anger formed inside him, and he became very restless.

Then he began to think about Nancy and the first time he had met her. He tried to analyze his reasons for being taken with her, but he could not, and he felt irritated with himself. She was no more beautiful or enchanting than many girls he had known in England, yet he could not forget her. He had never before encountered a lady or wench whom he had not been able to forget at will. It was possible, he decided, that her attractiveness and seductive wiles were blinding him to the truth about her. Then he suddenly realized that Nancy was the key to exposing Theodore, and he was determined, no matter the cost, to have her willingly or reluctantly assist him in seeking the justice he so desperately wanted.

---

After reading the general's letter, a shocked Irene sat very still in her chair while attempting to process the information. She knew that the contents of the letter had to be kept a secret to prevent ruining the life of her precious niece, Margaret Ann. She rose from her chair and walked over to the fireplace and tossed the letter into the fire.

Instead of waiting for the fire to consume the entire letter, Irene left the drawing room and headed upstairs. Nancy entered the room and hurried to the fireplace and successfully retrieved the letter. Most of it was still intact. She read it quickly, and with an evil delight, she took the letter and retreated to her bedroom upstairs.

In her bedroom, Nancy closed the door behind her. Then she went to a desk, opened the top drawer, and removed the leather box that she had taken from the ruins of her home in Annapolis Royal. She opened the box and placed the letter inside next to a gold medallion.

*Oh, my beloved Theodore, you will be so proud of me,* she thought. *We now have two powerful possessions that will be very useful in destroying our enemies, including that bastard Richard Hayes. Things are going better than we could have ever imagined.* And she laughed while holding onto the leather box.

# Chapter 19

With the war now officially over, two companies of regular English troops were stationed in Boston, but would soon either be sent home or to the Ohio Valley to protect the borders east from Indian attacks. A local military organization called the Boston Cadets, founded nearly three years earlier upon the recommendation of Governor Fenton, had proved to be very efficient in guarding the city and keeping local order.

The common room of the Fairview Tavern was crowded. Well-dressed merchants and ship owners drinking ale and hot spiced wines were discussing plans to expand their businesses now that the war had ended. They believed this was the perfect time for expansion and extensive travel throughout the colonies and the frontier.

Some of the men were drinking heavily, joking, and teasing a pair of tavern maids who were too busy to appreciate the attention they were receiving.

Had it not been for the English accents of the colonies and the somber dress of the men in the common room, Richard might have imagined himself back in England. The hickory fire burning in the hearth, the scrubbed pine tables, and even the sand on the floor reminded him of home. But no amount of wishful thinking would suddenly transport him there, and he forced himself to return to reality and focus on getting Theodore to confess.

After finishing his meal, Richard put on his greatcoat. He wanted to go to the Wentworth Mansion to confront Nancy this very day.

When he stepped outside, a light snow was falling, and a brisk wind from the west whipped the tiny flakes through the air. The flakes stung Richard's face, numbed his hands, and fell inside his collar, but he ignored the physical discomforts as he walked down the street. He was silently cursing the violation of loyalty and the inconsistency of women. The lifelong attitude he had maintained toward them as taught to him by his father, until he had met Nancy, was the right one, he told himself bitterly. He felt that any man who allowed himself to develop deep feelings for a woman, or any man who made the mistake of telling a woman candidly that he was in her hands, deserved the disdainful or cavalier treatment she would inevitably bestow upon him.

What disturbed Richard about Nancy was that she had given him every indication of responding to him as he had to her. He believed that the feelings for him that she had demonstrated had been genuine. There was no valid reason for her to play him for a fool, or was there? He considered that an ambitious young woman who was trying to better her social and financial position might want to marry a man from the aristocracy or wealthy class. But he felt that Nancy knew that due to his present circumstances he could do little or nothing for her. He continued to torture himself by asking the same two questions repeatedly in his mind: what possible cause did she have to pretend to feel affection for him while enticing him with her attractive and seductive physical appearance, and why did he feel that she was hiding something from him?

By the time Richard reached the Wentworth Mansion, the light snow had ceased, but the cold wind continued to brush up against his cheeks and send a nasty chill through his body.

He was greeted at the door by a maid who took his hat and greatcoat. Then he went into the drawing room and warmed his hands by the hearth while the maid went to get Nancy.

A few minutes later, Nancy appeared in the room. She stood facing Richard while digging her fingernails into the palms of her hands. He walked toward her, and their eyes met, and neither one wanted to be the first to look away.

"Why have you called upon me?" she asked. "Is it to interrogate me about why I was at the Dustin estate the night you were in pursuit of Theodore Blakeslee, or are you here to inform me of the outcome of today's hearing?"

Richard told her what had happened at the hearing and that Theodore was in jail under a doctor's care and the watchful eye of the constable. Then he changed the subject by telling her he did not accept her reason for being at the Dustin estate and demanded the truth.

Nancy was persistent in sticking to her story. "Why don't you believe me?" she asked. "What do I have to gain by not telling the truth, and why are you so obsessed with pursuing this ridiculous matter?"

He saw tears well up in her eyes, and he hesitated, but then pressed on firmly.

"Just tell me the truth, because I have a feeling that you are protecting someone, like that scoundrel Theodore Blakeslee."

There was a long silence, and she seemed to go through a great inner struggle before she found her voice. Then she adamantly warned Richard to stay away from Theodore and if possible leave Boston and settle in another colony under a new name and profession.

Richard's self-control snapped, and moving toward her, he put his arms around her and drew her to him. Nancy did not resist him, and for a moment she quietly accepted his embrace. Then she lifted her arms and clung to him too. She was trembling, and his hold tightened as he kissed her. However, he was surprised that her passion did not match his own.

Suddenly, Nancy put the heels of her hands against Richard's shoulders, shoved him away from her, and burst into tears. He stood very still while staring at her in astonishment.

"It is better we no longer see each other," she said. "Whatever passionate feelings and desires we have shared in the past are now gone. I want you to leave my sight this instant."

Before he could reply, Nancy ran from the room, sobbing.

Richard was stunned and remained motionless until the sound of her footsteps faded away as she raced up the stairs to her room. He was angry and hurt by her actions, but he was certain of one thing: that she and Theodore were somehow connected. And he was determined to learn the truth, if not from Nancy, then from Theodore.

With a grim look on his face, he quickly donned his greatcoat and hat and made his departure. As he walked out the door, Nancy emerged at the top of the stairs and exchanged her tears for laughter.

---

Before returning to the Fairview Tavern, Richard went straight to the jail. Upon his arrival, he found the constable and jailer lying unconscious on the floor. When he went to Theodore's cell to check on him, he found the cell door wide open and Theodore no longer there.

---

At the Wentworth Mansion, it was a cold and peaceful evening. The sun had faded into the horizon, and darkness had engulfed the land. The servants were preparing for supper. Nancy had taken to her room and was not seen since the early afternoon. William and Georgiana were preparing to go out, as they had been invited to dine at the home of Reverend and Mrs. Hartley.

Irene reassured her brother that she would dine with Margaret Ann and Nancy while keeping company with them. She had managed to get Black Crow back to the stables without anyone suspecting a thing. She knew that time was running out and he would have to return to the frontier despite Margaret Ann's strong objection.

After William and Georgiana had left for the evening, Irene was sitting in the drawing room, digesting the information contained in General Wolfe's letter and pondering the situation concerning Black Crow.

Irene's solitude was interrupted by a maid, who announced the arrival of a Sergeant Conroy and two soldiers. The sergeant removed his officer's hat, as did the other two soldiers upon their entrance into the room. Irene was gracious and inquired about their visit to her brother's home. She also informed the men that her brother and his wife were out for the evening.

Sergeant Conroy explained that he was returning from the Kingston settlement, where nearly three days earlier a group of Huron Indians had launched a vicious attack but were defeated by his militia. He explained that there was reason to believe that a handful of Huron warriors might have escaped and could be in the area. The sergeant and his men were going door to door to warn the people who lived on the outskirts of Boston to be on their guard.

Irene smiled while trying not to reveal what she knew about Black Crow. She thanked the sergeant and his men for their concern and promised them that she would alert her brother and also the entire household staff. Then she invited the men to dine with her, but they graciously declined her invitation and told her they had a few more places to visit before going into the city.

After they left, Irene quickly wrapped a heavy wool shawl around her shoulders and went to the stables. With a lantern in her hands to light the way through the darkness, she hurried along the muddy path. Suddenly, without warning, Nancy appeared in her midst.

"What are you doing out here, Miss Graham?" asked a startled Irene.

"I should be asking you the same question. It is not safe out here, especially with a Huron warrior hiding in the stables. Your niece should associate with the locals, not the savages," said Nancy in a sarcastic tone.

Irene pretended to be unaware of what Nancy was talking about. Nancy laughed for a moment and then revealed that she knew all about Margaret Ann giving shelter to the Huron warrior, perhaps the same one that Sergeant Conroy and his men were searching for. She boldly admitted to Irene that out of concern for everyone in the Wentworth household, she told the sergeant and his men where Margaret Ann was hiding her savage friend.

"You foolish woman, what have you done?" shouted a frantic Irene.

Before Irene could utter another word, loud screams were heard coming from the direction of the stables. Both Irene and Nancy hurried down the path, which was surrounded by barren trees and lightly snow-covered bushes. When they arrived at the stables, two soldiers were binding Black Crow's hands behind his back, and Sergeant Conroy was forcefully holding a tearful and frightened Margaret Ann.

"Stop your fussing, you Indian lover. We are going to deliver swift justice to this savage. And for your punishment, we will make you watch," said a vindictive Sergeant Conroy.

After the men had bound Black Crow's hands, one of the soldiers took out a knife and placed it to Black Crow's throat. The warrior struggled while the soldiers taunted him and spit in his face.

"Let him go this instant," demanded Irene. "He has done nothing wrong, and your behavior is unbecoming that of soldiers sworn to serve His Majesty and protect his subjects. My brother William has great influence in this colony, and he will see to it that you are brought up on murder charges if you carry out your vicious act."

"Aunt Irene, please don't let them kill Black Crow," pleaded a tearful Margaret Ann.

Sergeant Conroy told Margaret Ann to be silent, and then informed Irene not to interfere with army business. Nancy looked on with delight while anticipating what the outcome would be.

Before Sergeant Conroy could utter another word, a feisty Margaret Ann bit his hand. He yelled in pain while releasing her from his grasp. She ran to Black Crow and stood in front of him.

Irene demanded that the soldiers release Black Crow and untie his hands. While the men carried out Irene's request, Margaret Ann ran up to her aunt and thanked her for her kind intervention.

An angry Sergeant Conroy took out his pistol and aimed it at Black Crow. As Margaret Ann stared in the sergeant's direction, she saw the pistol and ran in front of Black Crow.

Irene screamed as the pistol was fired, and her niece collapsed at Black Crow's feet with blood streaming from her gown.

# Chapter 20

After hearing the loud screams and the gunshot, several of the servants descended upon the stables. A disoriented Sergeant Conroy dropped the pistol and stood motionless as a result of his careless and brutal act. Black Crow lifted a wounded Margaret Ann into his arms and followed Irene and some of the servants back to the mansion. Irene instructed the male servants to keep an eye on Sergeant Conroy and his men. She then sent another servant to Huntington Hall to seek the assistance of Dr. Thomas Gage.

Black Crow carried Margaret Ann into the house and upstairs to her room, where he placed her on the bed. Irene removed her shoes, and they tried to make her as comfortable as possible. The wound kept bleeding, and Margaret Ann's complexion was very pale. Black Crow tore off a piece of the drape hanging on the window and wrapped it tightly around her leg in an attempt to stop the bleeding. His efforts seemed to be working and would serve as a temporary solution until Dr. Gage's arrival.

Irene watched in awe as Black Crow attended to her niece while remaining calm. As Irene stared at him, she did not see a bloodthirsty, uncivilized savage, but a kind and compassionate man.

While the entire household was in an upheaval, Nancy hurried to her room. She picked up her leather box and enlisted one of the servants to assist her in carrying a small trunk to the carriage. Then she asked the carriage driver to take her to the Hancock Inn. As the carriage pulled away, Nancy pulled down the curtain on her carriage window, and she rested against the fine upholstered seat with the leather box on her lap.

---

At Huntington Hall, Martha and her son, Thomas, were sitting at the dining room table enjoying a delicious meal of chicken and cold ham with green peas and carrots. There was no exchange of conversation between mother and son. After a short while, Martha, unable to bear the silence any longer, spoke.

"My dear Thomas, the Wentworth Ball is nearly upon us. I do believe that it will be a grand affair. Are you planning to take anyone with you? I'm certain that William and Georgiana would not mind if you brought a young lady as your guest."

"I'm already bringing a guest, and that person would be you. My beloved mother, you shall be the prettiest and most elegant woman present, and I'm certain I will be the envy of all the gentlemen at the ball," replied Thomas with a grin.

Their pleasant conversation was interrupted by Mrs. Fitch, who handed Thomas a note from Irene Kent. Thomas read the note quickly and then rose from his Chippendale chair and went to get his medical bag.

Martha hurried after her son to inquire about the reason for the urgency. He told her that Margaret Ann had been shot and his medical expertise was needed immediately.

Upon hearing the news, Martha was stunned. She then put on her bonnet and overcoat, and went with Thomas to the Wentworth Mansion.

---

Richard walked the cobblestone streets of Boston for nearly two hours, searching for Theodore, but his search proved futile. He also went to Theodore's home. However, according to the servants, he had not been there. Two officers were assigned to stand guard at the Blakeslee residence in case he should return.

The constable and the jailer were examined by a physician who found that they had only suffered mild concussions from nasty blows to the head. The constable explained that Theodore seemed to be in a deep sleep when they entered his cell to check on him. But then he suddenly attacked the jailer and then the constable before making his escape. By this point, Richard felt certain that the shaking, trembling, and fainting that occurred in court had been a charade by Theodore to disrupt the hearing and allow him time to plan his next move.

Tired and hungry from his search, Richard returned to the Fairview Tavern. He sat at a table in the far corner, away from the crowd, and enjoyed a hot bowl of stew and a mug of ale. Then he went upstairs to his room to get a good night's sleep. He planned to rise at dawn and continue his search. Richard was determined to find Theodore and bring this awful episode in his life to a conclusion.

As he approached his room, he noticed that his door was open. When he entered, there were several candles lit and Nancy was sitting in a provocative manner on his bed. She stared at a surprised Richard and told him to close the door behind him. After closing the door, he went up to Nancy and placed his hands around her thin neck. Although she gasped a bit, she revealed no sign of fear in her eyes.

"What are you doing here? And where is Theodore Blakeslee?" asked Richard in a rough tone.

Nancy gave him a smile while shrugging her shoulders. As Richard began to lose his patience with her, he heard footsteps from behind. Then he turned around and saw Theodore standing in his path, pointing a pistol at his head.

# Chapter 21

Richard stood motionless as Theodore held a pistol to his head. Then he boldly demanded that Theodore put the pistol away. Theodore mocked him and told him that he was in no position to demand anything. Nancy smiled at Richard and then abruptly rose from the bed before slapping Richard in the face.

"That was for my sister whose heart you broke and whose life you ruined," replied a scornful Nancy. "My younger sister loved you with every fiber in her body, and you returned her affections with betrayal and humiliation."

Taken aback by Nancy's allegations and having difficulty recalling Nancy's sister, Richard asked for further details. Nancy stared at him disdainfully while revealing her sister's tragic story.

"It has been nearly ten years since the day my sister, Faith, came running through the meadows at our home in Hartfordshire, England, elated about meeting a young soldier who was serving in His Majesty's Army. She described the young soldier as extremely handsome and smartly dressed in his army uniform. Every day she met the young soldier at a local inn for a light meal and good company. Then one day the young soldier did not appear. My poor sister became concerned and went to search for him only to find him in an alley embracing and kissing another woman. Distraught and humiliated over her findings, she returned home with a broken heart."

As Nancy continued with her story, Richard began to remember a young woman named Faith who he shared a companionship with while in the army in England. He recalled that she was a sensitive girl with a kind smile.

"What happened to Faith?" asked a curious Richard.

"Two days later she drowned herself in the lake not far from our home. My parents were devastated, and they too died a few years later. My mother died from the fever, and my father was killed in a fight at a local tavern. Left with no family and no desire to remain in Hartfordshire or England because of the painful memories, I sold the family homestead and all its belongings, and I immigrated to Nova Scotia, where I made my home at Annapolis Royal. I would still be there if the French had not destroyed that beautiful place. Now do you remember my sister, or is she still unknown in your mind?" cried Nancy.

Theodore interrupted by revealing that he met Nancy when the ship he was sailing passage on to the colonies stopped briefly for supplies at Annapolis Royal. He confided in her about his swindling of money from a pathetic young soldier and that he was on his way to the colonies to start a new life.

When Theodore revealed Richard's name to Nancy, she became interested in joining him in his plan to go to Massachusetts Bay and win the heart of Sarah Dustin, the only daughter of George Dustin. Theodore planned to marry Sarah, and later on, with Nancy's assistance, steal the Dustin fortune while in the meantime continuing to swindle other unsuspecting colonists out of their money. Unfortunately, Zachary Carr, a potential investor, saw through Theodore's plan and was going to expose him. Therefore, Theodore killed him and blamed the attack on local Indians by setting fire to Carr's home and leaving a tomahawk embedded in the front door.

As Richard took in all that they had said, a triumphant Theodore sat in the only chair in the room while putting his pistol down next to him on the oak floor. Then he removed from his pocket a small, golden snuffbox engraved with his initials, and he opened the lid and took a generous pinch. He boasted about having Sarah under his spell through the use of a gold medallion that he had stolen from a merchant aboard the vessel to the colonies. The merchant insisted that the medallion was part of a buried treasure discovered by sailors on one of the islands. Legend had it that many years earlier it had belonged to a powerful chief who practiced black magic and used the medallion to lure young virgins, who he later sacrificed to the pagan gods.

"My plan was coming together quite nicely," said Theodore. "When that coward, George Dustin, tried to put a wedge between Sarah and me, I blackmailed him for Zachary Carr's death. I had no further trouble from him until you befriended George after saving his daughter's life. From that moment on, you have been a thorn in my side. You must thank Nancy for her intervention, which stopped me from killing you the first time I saw you at the docks," continued Theodore. "By the way, whether you believe me or not, I am not the one who tried to kill you shortly upon your arrival to this very room. But now I shall finish what someone else had attempted to do."

Thinking quickly, Richard grabbed hold of Nancy and pushed her onto Theodore. A furious Theodore threw Nancy to the floor while attempting to reach for his pistol. Richard removed the pistol from his belt and aimed it at Theodore. Nancy rose to her feet as Richard fired a shot at his enemy, but missed. Then, Theodore deliberately toppled over two of the lit candles, and the room became engulfed in flames. He then attempted to leave the room when a frightened Nancy tried to follow him.

"You are of no use to me any longer," said Theodore. "Go to your sister, Faith, and your parents."

Then he shot her before making his escape.

A mortally wounded Nancy clutched her side in agony. As she slumped to the floor, Richard grabbed a hold of her. Nancy's green eyes stared into the eyes of the man she tried to destroy, and she spoke in a low voice.

"You have to save Sarah Dustin from Theodore. I did not know that he was so evil. I forgive you for hurting my sister. Please, forgive me," she said as she moved her red lips to Richard's face.

In her final act, she managed to give him a peck on the cheek, and then she closed her eyes forever.

An upset Richard held Nancy in his arms and carried her out of the burning room. He made his way downstairs to the common room, where several men were carrying buckets of water upstairs in an attempt to extinguish the fire. To avoid the commotion, Richard carried Nancy out into the night air where he placed her body on the cold ground. He found himself staring at a woman, who was beautiful, lively, brave, and seductive, but foolishly allowed hatred, revenge, and the empty promises of a villain to lead her to a tragic demise.

"May God have mercy on your soul, and I am sorry for hurting Faith," uttered a sorrowful Richard while looking up at the sky.

---

When they arrived at the Wentworth Mansion, Thomas and Martha found the presence of commotion, confusion, and chaos everywhere. The constable and his men were escorting Sergeant Conroy and two militia men outside the mansion and back to the city. A frantic Irene was waiting impatiently in the great hall for Thomas. The servants were hurrying up and down the stairs, carrying fresh linens and basins of water. The housekeeper was sitting at the bottom of the staircase, weeping.

When they entered, Irene was relieved to see Thomas and Martha. After Thomas removed his coat and hat, Irene escorted him upstairs to Margaret Ann's room. Martha remained downstairs to avoid getting in the way. Before Thomas entered Margaret Ann's room, Irene gave him a brief account of what had taken place, and she warned him about Black Crow. However, she told Thomas that Black Crow had been very helpful in attending to her niece.

A maid servant opened the door to Margaret Ann's room, and Irene and Thomas, with his medical bag in his hands, went inside. Thomas walked over to the bed and examined Margaret Ann. A protective Black Crow watched intensely. After examining the wound and recognizing the large amount of blood loss, Thomas knew that the bullet would have to be surgically removed and that time was critical. He commented on the way someone had attempted to stop the bleeding with a piece of drapery. Irene gladly gave Black Crow credit for the deed.

Thomas washed his hands in a basin by the bed. Then he asked Irene to remain outside, and Black Crow to remain as his assistant. He also asked for two maids to remain nearby to assist with bringing basins of fresh water as needed.

Once the room was cleared, Thomas struck up a brief conversation with Black Crow, whose English and knowledge of attending bullet wounds impressed him. Then he opened his medical bag and took out a small vile of opiate, which he administered to Margaret Ann. Within a few minutes, she was in a deep sleep as Black Crow gently stroked her forehead.

With the assistance of the maids, they removed Margaret Ann's gown, leaving only her undergarments. Then Thomas took hold of his scalpel, the same one that he used to extract bullets from many wounded soldiers at Fort Wilderness, including General Kent's son, and he began to cut into the flesh of the left thigh. As he dug in search of the foreign object, blood trickled slowly from the wound. The bullet was deeply embedded, and Thomas skillfully tried not to let it break apart. As he continued with the delicate task, his scalpel glistened in the candlelight, and he was concerned about Margaret Ann's very pale complexion and the extent of damage caused by the bullet, which could possibly affect her ability to walk properly.

Downstairs in the drawing room, Irene was worried, and Martha did her best to comfort her.

When the housekeeper brought in a tray of tea, Irene remembered that William and Georgiana, who were dining at the home of Reverend Hartley, needed to be told of the situation. So she instructed the housekeeper to send word by one of the servants. Martha dutifully poured a cup of tea and gave it to Irene, who was seated in a wing chair by the hearth.

"Thank you, my dear friend," said Irene. "Thank God your Thomas had returned from Fort Wilderness and was here to save my precious niece. I would trust her life to no other surgeon in this entire colony. My husband wrote to me about the wonderful work Thomas had done in saving our Cooper. Thomas has a rare and special gift."

Martha smiled as her chest swelled with pride. She thanked Irene for her sincere compliment, and then a curious Martha asked what caused Margaret Ann's present dilemma. Irene took a few sips of her tea before telling her friend the entire story. She made certain to include Nancy's involvement, which indirectly led to the tragic shooting.

After Irene had finished speaking, Martha admitted that she had never trusted or approved of Nancy Graham.

"From the first time I laid eyes on that young woman, I felt she was trouble. Her mesmerizing green eyes and seductive wiles remind me of a harlot or Queen Jezebel," said Martha adamantly. "Is she still residing here?"

"I haven't seen her since Margaret Ann was shot. I assume she has retreated to her room and is remaining there in solitude."

At that moment, one of the servants came in with a tray of food, and Irene inquired about Nancy. The servant told her that Nancy had taken some of her belongings and that the carriage driver, Preston, had taken her back to the Hancock Inn. Martha commented that Nancy had been very ungrateful and inconsiderate to leave without saying good-bye or waiting for the outcome of Margaret Ann's predicament. Irene agreed and told Martha that it was for the best that she had gone.

Time seemed to pass very slowly as Irene and Martha waited for Thomas or one of the servants to bring news of Margaret Ann's condition. To help pass the time, Irene filled Martha in on the gossip at St. James' Court and the latest fashions in London. They managed to even laugh a bit, which helped to calm Irene's shattered nerves.

William and Georgiana soon came home and were beside themselves with worry and grief over Margaret Ann. But they were happy to see their friend Martha. While they waited, Irene told them the entire story. They were surprised and disappointed in Nancy, and shocked about Margaret Ann's friendship with Black Crow. William was very disturbed by Sergeant Conroy's behavior and promised to pursue the matter with Governor Fenton in the morning.

"What are we to do about our niece's attachment to a savage?" cried Georgiana. "This cannot be allowed, even if he has been kind and attentive to our beloved Margaret Ann. She will subject us to scandal, and we shall all be ruined. Oh, that poor girl. What will become of her and us?"

"My dear wife, let's not think about any unpleasant things at this moment," said William. "Let us hope that Margaret Ann shall survive this ordeal, and then we will deal with the matter of Black Crow later."

Irene agreed with her brother and told everyone present to keep good thoughts while reminding them that Margaret Ann was in the skillful and competent hands of Dr. Thomas Gage. Martha, who was pleased with Irene's confidence in her son, smiled as she poured tea for William and Georgiana. Georgiana accepted a cup and sipped it quietly, but William declined and decided to take a turn about the room. A short time later, Thomas came downstairs and entered the drawing room. Upon seeing him, everyone turned their attention to him. They all remained silent as an exhausted Thomas stared at them, speechless, with the look of deep concern in his eyes.

# Chapter 22

After regaining his ability to speak, Thomas explained to Margaret Ann's family and his mother that he was successful in removing the bullet; however, Margaret Ann had lost a considerable amount of blood. He continued to explain that the damage from the bullet could affect her use of the leg, but his biggest concern at the moment was infection.

"I do not mean to trespass on your kind hospitality, but it is most convenient for me to remain here tonight if Margaret Ann should need my immediate attention than to be some miles away," said Thomas.

William and Georgiana agreed and told Thomas that if he needed anything, they would make certain he had it. Georgiana said he could stay in the room across from Margaret Ann's and he should ring for the servants if he needed something.

"Our home is your home, and our household staff is at your disposal," said William. "My wife and I are in your debt for what you are doing for our precious niece. May we see her?"

"Yes, you may peek in on her, but do not remain very long. She is sleeping peacefully," replied Thomas.

Margaret Ann was in a deep sleep from the opiate, and Black Crow was attending to her. Thomas complimented Black Crow for his assistance and attentiveness.

"I am truly amazed at the helpfulness of that savage," said Thomas. "He appears to have strong affection for Margaret Ann, and I believe that his presence will be the perfect medicine in restoring her back to health. I do not intend to interfere with your relationship with your niece, but would it be possible for Black Crow to remain here until Margaret Ann is well again?"

William and Georgiana looked at each other disapprovingly, but they wanted their niece to make a full recovery. So upon Thomas's trusted recommendation they reluctantly agreed to temporarily have Black Crow reside at their home. Then they excused themselves and went upstairs.

Thomas told his mother that there was no need for her to remain any longer and she could take her leave. Before Martha left, Thomas asked her to have a servant bring him a change of clothes in the morning. She nodded her head, embraced Irene and then her son, and departed.

An exhausted Thomas sat down in a wing chair, and Irene brought him a cup of tea. As he sipped his tea, Irene told him the entire story involving Margaret Ann and Black Crow, and she also told him about Nancy and the events leading up to the unfortunate incident.

Thomas was shocked by Nancy's actions. He asked to see her, but Irene informed him that she had left and returned to the Hancock Inn.

After finishing his tea, Thomas excused himself and went upstairs to be with his patient, leaving Irene alone in the drawing room. She sat down on the divan, bowed her head, and began to pray for her niece's recovery and a solution to the situation involving Black Crow. Some time later, she picked up her head to find Black Crow present in the room, standing silently and staring at her.

"I did not mean to disturb you, but Bright Eyes' aunt and uncle insisted I leave the room. The good doctor told me to do as they requested and to go downstairs to find you. He said that when Margaret Ann awakes, he will send for me."

Irene was intrigued by the name Bright Eyes. When she commented on it, he explained that Margaret Ann's bright blue eyes reminded him of a crystal blue stream running through the forest. He also said that she was prettier than any squaw he had ever seen, and he admired her bravery and loyalty.

"My niece is very special to me and this entire family. We have only her best interest at heart. Thank you for all you have done for her. Dr. Gage praised you for your efforts," said a grateful Irene. "Tell me something. If it would be possible by some miracle that you and Bright

Eyes, my niece, could be together, would you love her and protect her?" inquired Irene as she stared at this breathtaking specimen of a man.

Black Crow replied with deep conviction and sincerity that he would protect Bright Eyes with his life. But, sadly, in his heart, he knew that society and Bright Eyes' family would not allow them to be together. He had resigned himself to the reality that he had to return to the frontier and his people. Irene politely smiled and offered him some food and drink, which he accepted. As he sat and ate, Irene began to formulate a plan that would benefit both Margaret Ann and Black Crow without the interference of anyone, including William and Georgiana. But she kept those thoughts to herself.

---

Richard remained with Nancy's body until a physician arrived to examine the corpse and officially pronounce her as deceased. The physician was a gray-haired gentleman wearing a black suit with silver buttons. In his right hand, he carried a cloth bag containing his medical equipment, and in his left hand he had a piece of paper: a death certificate. After briefly examining Nancy's lifeless body, he pronounced that she was dead and then went inside to fill out the death certificate. Then he went back outside and carefully wrapped Nancy's body in white linen and took her away in a wagon to the icehouse, where she would remain until burial.

Feeling sorry for Nancy and the fact that she had no family, Richard informed the physician that he would give the deceased a decent Christian burial. After settling matters with the physician, Richard returned to the charred remains of his room above the tavern. The tavern owner was not pleased with the damage but was relieved that the fire had been contained to only Richard's quarters.

The constable soon arrived to investigate the situation. After Richard had given his statement, the constable hurried to the Governor's Mansion to inform Governor Fenton of what had taken place and to have the governor issue a warrant for the arrest of Theodore Blakeslee.

Richard went to the Hancock Inn to search Nancy's room in the hope of finding something that would lead him to Theodore's whereabouts. When he arrived at the inn, the common room was filled with tradesmen and merchants celebrating the end of the war. He made his way through the crowd and loud voices, and hurried upstairs.

Upon entering Nancy's room, Richard discovered that the door was slightly ajar, so he approached cautiously. When he went inside, he found that the room had been ransacked. The drawers of the high boy had been opened and clothes had been thrown about the room. The bed had been moved, and other pieces of furniture had been disturbed. He searched the room, but he found that nothing seemed to be missing.

Then he remembered the leather box that Nancy had taken from the ruins of her home at Annapolis Royal. He looked intensely for the box, but his effort was futile. He believed that Theodore had ransacked Nancy's room, searching for the box. Two questions stalked Richard's mind: *does Theodore have the box, and what does it contain?* As he pondered these questions, he stared into the mirror above the dressing table and he saw an image of Sarah Dustin. He quickly and frantically hurried downstairs and out into the streets. He rode on horseback, making his way to the Dustin estate, fearing that he would find the villainous Theodore there.

# Chapter 23

Richard's mind was plagued with the possible dangers that Sarah would be facing while in the clutches of his evil nemesis, Theodore. He had come to the realization that although he had felt the unreasonable surge of lust to kill the enemy during war, his hatred was now motivated by revenge and the desperate attempt to save an innocent life. Richard knew that war had not only stripped him of romance and glamour, but had led him into a ruthless existence filled with inevitable danger that was no longer attractive to him. And he realized that he was faced with an uncertain and terrifying battle between good and evil, a fight that he prayed would end in good triumphing over evil.

When he had finally reached his destination, an anxious and perspiring Richard dismounted his horse, quickly hurried to the front door, grabbed hold of the door knocker, and banged loudly and furiously for someone to answer. He waited impatiently for a response, but no one came to the door. Then he attempted to open the door, but it was locked. Overcome with fear and desperation, he ran to the side of the mansion, nearly tripping over his own feet. When he reached the terrace, he found that the doors of the drawing room were open and a strong wind was blowing inside.

Upon entering the drawing room, he found a shaken Mabel Dustin slumped in a Chippendale chair, frantically mumbling words that he could not clearly understand.

Richard took a firm hold of her and asked what had happened. Mabel seemed a bit incoherent and cried out to Sarah. When he inquired about Sarah, Mabel just stared at him while continuously uttering her daughter's name. Then he heard voices coming from outside the room. He left Mabel and rushed into the great hall. Upon approaching the grand staircase leading to the second floor, he saw George Dustin arguing with Theodore Blakeslee. Richard shouted to the two men while climbing up the stairs.

"Richard, please help me save my beloved daughter from this wicked man," yelled George. "Theodore has come to take my Sarah far away with him, never to return."

"It is time that I silence this worthless fool. Richard, you are too late to save your pathetic friend, and his daughter is all mine," Theodore shrieked.

To Richard's horror, Theodore suddenly plunged a knife into George's chest and pushed him down the stairs. Richard positioned himself tightly against the wall as George's body tumbled to the bottom of the stairs. Theodore disappeared into the shadows of the upper floor while laughing. Richard hurried to examine a mortally wounded George.

Gently turning George onto his side, Richard listened as the dying man spoke to him.

"I dismissed the servants for a few days. My wife and I were attending to Sarah. All seemed peaceful until I came upstairs to look in on Sarah and I had to thwart Theodore from entering her room. Unfortunately, he has gotten the better of me. Please save my daughter and stop that madman. The medallion gives him power. You must take it from him and destroy it in order to stop him. Please act quickly before he claims another innocent life," uttered George while grasping Richard's arm.

He took a final gasp of breath and then fell silent with his eyes wide open. A remorseful Richard closed the dead man's eyes and remained immobile for a few moments. It had been less than twenty-four hours since he stood over Nancy Graham's body. Now it was George. Both Nancy and George had been murdered by his former friend Theodore, a swindler turned kidnapper and murderer.

When Richard regained his senses, all he could think of was poor, helpless Sarah. His great worry for Sarah caused large amounts of adrenaline to rush through his body, causing him to hurry like a mountain cat up the stairs. He searched the entire floor, including

Sarah's bedroom, but he did not find Sarah or Theodore. Then Richard found a blue ribbon on the floor, which he thought must have fallen out of Sarah's hair.

"I will find you, Sarah, and I will save you from that monster. I swear my life on it, and your father's soul," shouted an angry and determined Richard while clutching the blue ribbon in his hand.

# Chapter 24

**Several days had passed** since Theodore had kidnapped Sarah. Richard, along with a small group of militia, diligently searched door to door throughout many neighborhoods. Unfortunately, their search was futile.

Governor Fenton issued a warrant for Theodore's arrest, and offered a generous reward.

Richard blamed himself for the deaths of Nancy Graham and George Dustin. His heart ached for Mabel Dustin, who was mourning the loss of her husband and frantically worrying about her daughter. The question that weighed heavily on many people's minds as well as Richard's was whether they would ever see Sarah Dustin again.

With the assistance of the constable and his men, Richard continued knocking on doors, making inquiries about whether anyone had seen a man who fit Theodore's description, with a young woman. But no one had seen either one of them.

Theodore's home and personal property had been confiscated, and he had little means, so what Richard wondered was what Theodore was depending on for resources and who could be assisting him.

"With no money or connections, how is he surviving?" Richard asked the constable. "It seems incredible that no one has seen Theodore or Sarah."

"Major Hayes, do not forget that Boston is a large city with many places to hide. I fear that Mr. Blakeslee is well concealed somewhere in the city. But do not fear, because he will soon be discovered and brought to justice for his crimes."

Richard tried desperately to obtain comfort from the constable's response, but he knew that he would not find peace until Sarah was found alive and well.

Exhausted from their search, the constable and his men returned to his quarters for a respite. Richard told the constable he would rejoin him and his men within an hour. Then Richard returned to the Fairview Tavern to rest and to have a light meal.

The tavern owner and his wife were very hospitable and generous to Richard. They treated him to a delicious meal of pork, ham, and salad, and they insisted on not taking payment for the meal. A grateful Richard thanked them for their kindness and then sat back in a wooden chair by the stone fireplace and removed his boots. He hid them under the table to avoid offending the other patrons for his lack of manners. While he was eating, the tavern owner's wife refilled his mug with ale and tried to reassure Richard that he would find Theodore and Sarah. She told him that she was praying for an end to this terrible situation and for Sarah to be found unharmed and reunited with her family.

After finishing his meal, Richard put his boots on and was preparing to rejoin the constable and his men when Joshua Pierce entered the tavern. Upon seeing Richard at the table, Joshua hurried over to him and demanded to speak to him. First he looked around the dining room, and then he spoke to Richard in a soft voice.

"I heard that you were looking for a man who had swindled you, and now he is wanted for murder and kidnapping by the authorities," said Joshua. "I know where he is hiding. And the young woman you are seeking is with him."

Richard rose to his feet, asking, "Where is he?"

Joshua calmly told Richard that Theodore was hiding aboard a ship owned by William Wentworth that would be leaving port the next day. He said that he would take Richard to the ship, but that Richard would have to accompany him alone. Although Richard realized Joshua's request seemed a bit odd, he agreed to go with him, as he was not afraid to face his nemesis and was willing to risk his life to save Sarah.

"I will follow you and honor your request, but you must take me to the ship at once," said Richard.

Joshua nodded in agreement and made his way to the front door.

Behind Joshua's back, Richard discreetly whispered to the tavern owner where he was going and told him to send word to the authorities to go to the docks immediately. The tavern owner carried out Richard's request while Richard and Joshua went on their way.

---

Georgiana Wentworth was descending the staircase when she saw her sister-in-law, Irene Kent, standing in the great hall. Georgiana was happy to see Irene, who she had not seen in a few days following her departure from the Wentworth home. To William and Georgiana's surprise, Irene had rented Stoke Lodge on the outskirts of Cambridge and had taken immediate occupancy.

Georgiana escorted Irene into the drawing room, where they sat on the sofa by the fireplace and engaged in friendly conversation.

"My dear Irene, I am so glad to see you. We all miss you terribly, especially Margaret Ann. Are you settled in, and how are you enjoying your new dwelling?" asked Georgiana.

"I am enjoying Stoke Lodge very much, and my newly hired servants have been wonderful in getting the place in order. I am patiently awaiting the arrival of more furniture from England, but the present furnishings will suffice for now," said Irene. "But that is enough about me. How is Margaret Ann doing?"

Georgiana explained that Margaret Ann was recovering nicely from the bullet wound and that Dr. Gage was very hopeful for a full recovery. Then she told Irene that Margaret Ann was very sad without Black Crow by her side.

"Although that savage had great compassion and attentiveness toward our beloved Margaret Ann, he had no place in our home, and their relationship had to end. Our family's reputation as well as Margaret Ann's was at stake. No love or friendship is worth the scandal and ruin of one's reputation and that of one's family," said Georgiana adamantly.

Georgiana continued by saying that William had given Black Crow a bag of silver coins and some food before sending him on his way, and that William along with two male servants accompanied Black Crow to the entrance of the forest not far from their home, and William warned Black Crow never to return.

"We knew that Black Crow's departure would devastate Margaret Ann, but we had no choice in the matter. We did Black Crow a favor by assisting him in escaping from Sergeant Conroy and his men. When Margaret Ann is well again, William and I are going to take her on holiday to London. The trip will do her good, and we hope it will make her forget about that blood-thirsty savage."

Irene was not surprised by her brother's actions or his wife's hurtful words. She reminded Georgiana that it was the hatred and vicious actions of Sergeant Conroy and his men that nearly got Margaret Ann killed, and it was Black Crow who indirectly saved Margaret Ann's life, and for that they should all be grateful. Georgiana did not wish to listen to Irene's praise of Black Crow any longer, so she changed the conversation by inquiring about General Kent and Cooper.

Their conversation was interrupted by William's entrance into the drawing room. He was not pleased to see his sister, but he carefully concealed his feelings by greeting her with a fake smile and hug. Georgiana politely excused herself and went upstairs to see Margaret Ann, leaving William and Irene alone.

After Georgiana had left, William closed the door. He then instructed Irene to be seated as he removed a letter from his coat pocket. Irene glared at her brother and the letter that he was holding. An uncomfortable feeling seized her body.

"My dear sister, do not pretend to be ignorant of the contents of this letter. You were careless in destroying it after receiving it from Lord Amherst a few weeks ago. Before he died, General Wolfe gave this wretched letter to his friend and instructed him to give it to you. The late general wanted to ease his conscience by revealing that he is Margaret Ann's father and that her mother is a slave from the islands. Our beautiful Margaret Ann, who we all love and cherish, is tainted with Negro blood. This terrible truth will make her an outcast to our society; and if her secret is discovered, it will bring ruin and disgrace not only upon her but all connected with her."

Before Irene could respond, William continued to speak and revealed that Nancy Graham found the letter that Irene had carelessly thrown into the fire, and kept it in her possession until her demise, upon which Theodore Blakeslee discovered it. With the letter in his possession, Theodore wasted no time in blackmailing William, asking

William to assist him in leaving the colonies with Sarah Dustin as his prisoner, in exchange for the letter.

"How could you have been so foolish as not to destroy this vile piece of paper?" asked William. "Luckily, Theodore's greed and desperate circumstances have allowed me to regain possession of it, and after tomorrow he will be gone from our lives, and the secret will be safe."

Then he told a shocked Irene that once Margaret Ann was able to travel, he and Georgiana would take her to London where they would make arrangements for her to have comfortable lodging and adequate financial means, and then return to Boston without her. He was hoping that Margaret Ann would become accustomed to London society and never want to return home. William believed it would be a blessing for Margaret Ann to be out of their presence.

"You are a selfish, uncaring, and cold-hearted bastard," shrieked Irene. "I cannot believe you are my brother. I love Margaret Ann as if she were my own daughter. I will not abandon her, and I will defend her until the day I die. I will not allow you to leave her alone in a large and unfriendly city where she will be vulnerable to unscrupulous individuals and opportunists. I want Margaret Ann to come to live with me, and Victor and I will see to it that she wants for nothing, including love and happiness. My mind is made up on the subject, and there will be no further discussion."

Knowing that his sister was stubborn and had a will of iron, William agreed to her request. He also felt relieved of the burden of caring for a young woman cursed with a dark secret.

Before she departed, Irene quickly rose from the sofa, snatched the letter from William, and tore it into pieces before tossing the remnants into the blazing fire. This time she watched closely, making certain that the pieces were consumed by the flames. William stared at his sister while she performed the task, and then walked over to a serving table and poured a glass of wine.

"Do you wish to join me in a toast to Margaret Ann's new life?" asked William.

Irene refused by saying, "I do not drink with swine, even if they happen to be my own flesh and blood. When Margaret Ann is able to travel, I will come for her and bring her to my new home. Do take care, my brother. Take very good care."

With a disappointed and disdainful expression on her face, Irene walked away from William. After Irene departed, William enjoyed his glass of wine.

---

Black Crow could not stay away from Margaret Ann. He disobeyed William's warning and returned to the mansion. Fortunately for Black Crow, Irene saw him before her brother did. She convinced him to accompany her back to Stoke Lodge where she offered the warrior shelter and refuge.

After leaving her brother's home, Irene returned to Stoke Lodge, where she hurried to the attic. Upon entering the drafty chamber, she greeted Black Crow, who was sitting on the floor. Irene told the good-looking warrior that very soon he would be reunited with the young woman he called Bright Eyes and that they would continue their friendship under her watchful eye. Black Crow looked at Irene with a puzzled expression.

"Do not worry, my savage friend," said Irene. "I shall transform you into a fine-looking English gentleman who will attract the attention of all the ladies and gentlemen of high society, especially the ones at St. James' Palace. Now, let us begin," said a very pleased and determined Irene.

---

When they had reached the docks, Richard followed Joshua to a large ship that was anchored at the far end of the pier. As they boarded the ship, Richard was shocked to see that it was the *Lonesome Mermaid.* Joshua put his index finger to his lips and motioned for Richard to go below deck. When Richard went below, he opened the door to the captain's quarters, but no one was present. As he attempted to ask Joshua where the captain and his crew were, Joshua quickly ran away. Suddenly, Theodore Blakeslee appeared in the doorway with a malevolent look on his face and two swords in his hands. Richard knew that this would be their final showdown.

# Chapter 25

"I shall cut you to ribbons," scowled Theodore. "Take this sword and let us begin. Only one of us shall leave this ship alive, and that someone will be me."

Richard was well aware of the dangerous situation he was facing, but he was determined to fight Theodore and crush him and his disdainful arrogance and evil intentions. Richard eyed his opponent while holding the sword in his hand.

"On guard," Theodore shouted.

The words were scarcely out of his mouth when Theodore leaped toward Richard, causing Richard to side-step to avoid a clumsy but ferocious blow. Theodore lunged a second time, and then a third, and Richard, turning aside the strokes along the length of his own blade with a quick, practiced wrist, realized he was indeed fighting a beginner. Nonetheless, Richard remained on the defensive. Theodore was dangerous in spite of his lack of style; his moves were unpredictable, and his hatred of Richard made him fixed on killing his enemy.

They circled each other twice, and the smug smile on Theodore's face was an indication that he thought he would surely win. Like so many men who held inflated opinions of themselves, Theodore seemed to feel that he was invincible, but Richard vowed that good would defeat evil. Theodore would not be satisfied with less than victory, and would certainly run Richard through if he lowered his guard.

At the moment there seemed to be no way out of the deadly dilemma. Richard knew that he could not continue to retreat indefinitely, and he was afraid that sooner or later one of Theodore's wild slashes might catch him off-balance. The blade of Theodore's sword came uncomfortably close twice, and Richard feared that even a man with a perfect sense of timing and a good eye might eventually slip. He quickly decided on deceiving his opponent by shifting to the offensive side. He thrust at Theodore three times in quick succession, making sure that he merely cut through the cloth of Theodore's white linen shirt.

It was gratifying for Richard to see Theodore's arrogance transform into dismay, but he tried to shut out the image of Theodore's pale and wicked face that stared at him. Richard knew that the duel had to end and that he had to defeat Theodore before Theodore had the opportunity to kill him. Richard also worried about how he would find Sarah if he killed Theodore. Suddenly, Richard forcefully moved forward, whipping his sword fiercely, causing Theodore to frantically defend himself. The pressure mounted as Richard crowded Theodore into an increasingly tight corner. Finally, Richard managed to slide his blade along the length of his adversary's blade, and he did not stop until the two weapons were locked, hilt to hilt. Then a quick, strong, upward thrust disarmed Theodore, and his sword flew across the cabin, landing several feet away.

An angry and desperate Theodore ran after his sword. He cursed while picking it up, and then whirled the blade and charged at Richard once more. Richard, who had not moved, met the renewed attack calmly, and repeated the same maneuver. This time Richard put more force into the assault, and Theodore's sword soared high into the air. After Theodore was disarmed, he fled in fright. Richard dropped his sword and hurried after Theodore, chasing him up on deck, where he trapped him in a corner of the ship's bow. In the meantime, the constable and his men had arrived.

Feeling like a trapped animal, Theodore removed a pistol, the same one he had used to shoot Nancy, from under his coat, and he aimed it at Richard. He stared Richard in the eyes.

"This is the end for you, my pathetic friend. You may have exposed me and foiled my plans, but I shall be the victor by sending you to hell," shrieked a vengeful Theodore.

As Richard stood defenseless in the presence of his enemy, a shot was fired. Richard flinched from the loud sound, and then, to his chagrin, Theodore collapsed. As Richard approached him, Theodore gave a last gasp for breath and died with his devilish eyes staring at Richard.

It was the constable who had fired the shot that killed Theodore, saving Richard's life.

The constable instructed his men to search the ship for Sarah Dustin. After Richard had regained his senses from the present ordeal, he assisted in the search.

After painstakingly searching the *Lonesome Mermaid* from top to bottom, they found a frightened Sarah tied up in the cargo hold of the ship. When Sarah saw Richard, she cried and begged him to take her home. The constable removed the rope from around her hands and feet, and Richard wrapped her in a blanket and carried her up on deck.

"You saved me once again from that demon. You are my hero," said a grateful Sarah as she rested in Richard's strong arms.

"You are safe," replied Richard. "Theodore Blakeslee can never harm you again. Now, I will take you home to your mother."

On the docks, two of the constable's men had arrested Joshua Pierce, who had tried to thwart them from going aboard the *Lonesome Mermaid*. Joshua kept his head down as Richard, with Sarah in his arms, walked past him. Richard was shocked that Joshua was involved with Theodore, and quickly dismissed unpleasant thoughts about Theodore by focusing his efforts on returning Sarah to her family. Richard was unaware William Wentworth was watching surreptitiously from nearby.

---

Martha Huntington Gage was sitting at her desk in the drawing room, writing a letter to her cousin, when her solace was interrupted by Thomas's entry into the room. He gave a polite greeting to his mother and quietly walked over to the fireplace and stared into the fire. He appeared to be deep in thought.

Acting as the concerned parent, Martha dispensed with her letter-writing and spoke to her son.

"You seem preoccupied this evening. What is on your mind?"

Thomas shrugged his shoulders and told his mother that it was nothing of importance to discuss. He walked to a serving table, poured a glass of sherry, and stood motionless with the glass in his hand.

Then without warning, he threw the glass into the fireplace, cursing Nancy Graham.

"How could that lovely woman have deceived me in such a cruel manner? Although I had only known her for a short time, I began to have feelings for her, and these feelings were leading me to gather the courage to establish a courtship with her. Because of her scheming and involvement with a criminal, which has led to her tragic demise, I have been left to feel like a fool with a broken heart."

As Martha tried to offer comfort to her son, he demanded that she change the conversation. He did not want to speak of Nancy Graham ever again.

Martha honored her son's wishes and began a conversation about Thomas's decision concerning General Kent's offer to work at the hospital in Cambridge. Thomas remained silent for a few moments and then informed Martha that after operating on Margaret Ann, he came to the realization that his calling was to heal the sick and the wounded.

"As much as you would hope for me to marry and give you heirs to carry on the Huntington Gage legacy, I must disappoint you by pursuing a career as a physician," he said. "Saving the lives of those in need will bring me comfort and a sense of accomplishment. And perhaps one day when I least expect it, I may fall in love with a wonderful woman who will marry me and bear me many children. Wouldn't that make you proud, my dear mother?"

Trying to hold back tears, Martha embraced her son and told him that she was very pleased with his decision to work at the hospital, and she pledged her full support and assistance. She also explained that in order to find love and be loved, a person must always keep an open heart, because when the heart is open, love will always find its way in.

"You have a special gift to heal, and you need to utilize that gift," she told him. "God rewards those who use their talents for good. I truly believe that your day of reward is forthcoming. Keep the faith and be patient, my son."

Thomas thanked his mother for her kind words of encouragement. Then he kissed her gently on the forehead before leaving the room.

As Thomas left her sight, Martha took a deep breath and was relieved that Thomas had made a wise choice. She also was grateful that Nancy Graham was no longer a part of his life and that the Gage family had been spared unspeakable heartache.

---

When the coach arrived at the Dustin estate, several servants came out to meet Richard and Sarah. Richard carried Sarah into the mansion, where they were greeted by a relieved and grateful Mabel, who was dressed in a black brocade gown.

"How is my precious angel? I am so happy to see my Sarah. Please, follow me and bring her upstairs," said Mabel as she led the way.

Upon hearing her mother's kind and gentle voice, Sarah opened her eyes and uttered, "Mother, it is wonderful to see you and to be back at the place I love very much. Where is Father? I wish to see his smiling face."

Mabel did not answer her daughter, because she did not want to upset Sarah by telling her the sad news about her father's death at the hands of Theodore Blakeslee. She told Sarah that her father had gone out and would return soon. As Richard carried Sarah up the staircase, he whispered pleasant thoughts to her. He reminded her that she was safe in the bosom of her family, and he promised her that he would never let anyone hurt her again.

After Sarah was settled in her room, Richard took from his coat pocket a blue ribbon and returned it to her.

"I do believe that this belongs to you. I found it on the floor of your room after Theodore had taken you away. The color blue is a majestic and pretty color that goes well with the beautiful young lady who wears it in her hair," said Richard with a smile.

Sarah thanked Richard as she took the ribbon from his hand. Then two servants entered with a basin of water, a tray of food, and extra blankets. Mabel insisted that her daughter freshen up and then have something to eat. At that moment, Richard decided to take his leave. He promised he would return in a few days for a visit.

After departing from the Dustin estate, Richard had a gut-wrenching feeling that this horrible ordeal was not yet over. While riding in the carriage, he leaned his head back against the soft upholstery and closed his eyes for a moment. He began to recall the night that someone wearing a mask tried to strangle him in his room at the

Fairview Tavern. He also thought about Theodore saying that he had not played a part in that attempt on Richard's life. Then he recalled George Dustin's words about William Wentworth's involvement in shipping and ownership of the *Lonesome Mermaid*, the same ship that Theodore and Sarah had been aboard. After pondering these facts, Richard decided to call upon William Wentworth, so he instructed the driver to take him to the Wentworth Mansion.

# Chapter 26

When he arrived at the Wentworth Mansion, Richard told the driver to wait for him. He knocked at the front door and saw someone move away from one of the windows. Then the housekeeper answered the door and let him inside. She led Richard to the drawing room, where he found Georgiana sitting in a chair, doing needlepoint. Georgiana stopped what she was doing and gave Richard a warm greeting as he entered the room. She told the housekeeper to bring a tray of tea and dessert to her guest. Richard politely declined the offer, and Georgiana dismissed the servant.

Richard did not engage in petty conversation, but instead proceeded to inquire about William. Georgiana graciously informed Richard that her husband was at the wharves, checking on his ships in preparation for their excursion to the West Indies.

"William left some time ago, and I do expect him to return shortly," said Georgiana. "Please stay and wait with me. I certainly could use the company."

Richard accepted the woman's invitation and began to fill her in on the events of the past several days. Georgiana was horrified by Theodore Blakeslee's actions, and she was relieved that Sarah Dustin was safe. She also expressed deep sorrow and astonishment over Nancy Graham's involvement with Theodore, which led to her demise as well as that of George Dustin.

"I am at a loss for words when it comes to the heinous behavior of human beings who show no regard for human life by allowing evil to dictate their lives," she said.

"I agree with you, my dear wife," replied William as he made his appearance into the drawing room. "These wicked individuals need to be brought to justice. I am pleased to announce that the people of Boston and this colony owe a debt of gratitude to Major Richard Hayes for thwarting these villains at the risk to his own life. My congratulations to you, major, for a job well done."

Georgiana rose from her chair and greeted her husband and then explained that Richard had come in search of him. William stared at Richard with a sly look, but played the gracious host by offering Richard a glass of wine, which he did not accept.

Their conversation was interrupted by the housekeeper, who informed Georgiana that her assistance was needed upstairs. Georgiana excused herself, leaving the two men alone.

Silence filled the room. Then Richard craftily began a conversation by inquiring how things were with William's ships. William replied by stating all was well and the ships' captains were preparing to leave in the morning for the West Indies.

"There is a demand for sugar and spices here in the colonies," said William. "I am obliged to fulfill that request, which will be very profitable."

"Does that obligation also involve aiding a criminal in the crimes of stealing, kidnapping, and murder?" Richard asked disdainfully.

"Major Hayes, I am shocked and confused by your statement. I am an honorable man with many purposes in life, one of which is to be a successful businessman in the New World."

Richard, tired of the cat and mouse game, admitted that he found Theodore aboard the *Lonesome Mermaid*. He also said that Sarah Dustin was found in the cargo and that a sailor by name of Joshua Pierce lured Richard to the ship, leaving him to face Theodore in a deadly sword fight that culminated in Theodore's death.

William desperately tried to compose himself and denied all knowledge of Richard's story.

Suddenly, the housekeeper interrupted once again by asking William for a letter opener. William told Richard to be patient while he went to the desk to get it. When William opened the desk, Richard saw a black mask, the same mask that the person who had tried to strangle him had been wearing. Richard remained calm and waited for the housekeeper to leave the room. Then he boldly stepped forward and reached into the desk, taking the mask into his hand and holding it in front of William's face.

"I do believe this belongs to you and the person who tried to kill me many nights ago. And I believe that person was you," shouted an angry Richard.

"Keep silent, you fool, for I do not want my wife or the servants to hear your wild accusations. You are terribly mistaken about me trying to strangle you," said William defensively.

"I never mentioned in what manner my attacker tried to kill me. The only way that you would have that information was if you were the one who was wearing this mask. It was you," said Richard.

"Yes. If it pleases you to be correct, I did try to strangle you the night of your arrival to Boston. And, yes, I was involved in helping Theodore with his attempt to leave the colonies with Sarah Dustin. My involvement in the kidnapping was revenge against George Dustin for his competitiveness in the shipping industry. He had been undermining me and making higher profits than me. It was unfair, because I was the one who had helped him to get established in the business, and he repaid my hard work and generosity by becoming more successful than me."

William continued by saying that he wanted George to suffer and the only way was to go after his daughter, which Theodore had been very instrumental in accomplishing. So William entered into a scheme with Theodore that William had believed would satisfy both men. Theodore would have Sarah and control of the Dustin fortune, and William would have his revenge upon George. Then he denied any involvement with Nancy Graham and said it was a sin for such a beautiful young woman to have been taken from life.

"I knew you were a threat from the moment I made your acquaintance at the Hancock Inn," said William. "I thought perhaps I could have done away with you privately or at least scare you into leaving for the fear of your life. But I misjudged you. You are fearless, and indeed a force not to be reckoned with. Congratulations, George Dustin. Even in death you have beaten me."

After William had finished speaking, Richard threw the mask on the floor and walked away in disgust. As Richard was leaving the room,

William called out to him and said he would go to the constable's office in the morning and make a full confession, which would ultimately lead to life in prison or a trip to the gallows.

An unsympathetic Richard walked into the hall and took a deep sigh of relief. The ordeal that began in London with Theodore swindling him and his associates and then culminating in kidnapping, revenge, and murder, had finally come to an end. At last, Richard could clear his name and live in peace.

Richard's train of thought was interrupted by Georgiana, who appeared in the hall with an elegantly dressed gentleman, who she introduced to Richard.

"Major Richard Hayes, this is Lord Jeffrey Amherst. He is a dear family friend who has come to inquire about our Margaret Ann," said Georgiana.

As Lord Amherst reached out to shake Richard's hand, Georgiana inquired about her husband. Before Richard could answer, they heard the shot of a pistol, which came from the drawing room.

Richard hurried into the room with Lord Amherst and a frightened Georgiana behind him. They found William slumped over in a chair with a bullet wound to his head, the smoking pistol in his lap, and the mask clenched in his left hand.

Lord Amherst went over to William, examined him, and then announced that he was dead. Richard shook his head, and Georgiana wept bitterly while Lord Amherst cunningly took the mask out of the dead man's hand and placed it in his coat pocket.

# Chapter 27

The cold March winds eventually surrendered to the warmth of spring and nature's promise of hope and rebirth. The flowers began to grow, the grass turned green and grew tall on the sprawling hills, and the new leaves on the trees rustled gently in the spring breeze. The crickets were chirping in nearby fields at night while the owls stayed perched on tree branches, acting as guardians of the forests at night. The deer, rabbits, beavers, and other animals had come out of hibernation and were roaming the vast woods and forests. The harsh and cold elements of winter had gone away, taking with them the doom and gloom of war, bloodshed, and revenge.

Peace and prosperity were flourishing throughout the colonies. Cities like Boston, Philadelphia, and New York were thriving with trade, and large numbers of immigrants were arriving daily to settle in the New World. Some went north, some went south, and others moved westward into the rugged and untamed frontier. The French were gone, and the Indian tribes were forced to live on the other side of the Appalachian Mountains or in Spanish-controlled Florida, leaving the English practically in complete control of the New World along the Eastern Seaboard.

A young and politically inexperienced monarch of twenty-two years old was sitting on the throne of England, and he was determined to fill his country's treasury with the profits from England's colonies. His greed, outrageous new laws, acts of taxation, and disregard for the colonists would eventually lead to chaos, turmoil, rebellion, and war. But for the present, things were quiet.

During the month of April, the colonists indulged in celebration as soldiers marched through the streets with large crowds cheering on the men who had served bravely in His Majesty's armed forces. Parties, balls, and assemblies were held almost everywhere, including local inns, taverns, and private homes. Shopkeepers and warehouse proprietors were busy making and selling elegant suits and gowns for men and women, especially those of high society.

The construction of beautiful homes, mansions, and public buildings were underway through the efforts of craftsmen, artisans, and builders. The port cities were crowded daily with ships sailing in and out, carrying goods and passengers. Roads and bridges were under construction, and those residing or coming to the New World had unthinkable opportunities. These were very good times.

As many rejoiced in celebration and hope of prosperity, there were some who suffered great financial burdens or personal losses. The Wentworth and Dustin families were slowly recovering from the losses of their patriarchs and the scandals that had affected their families. George Dustin had been buried in the cemetery of Christ Church, with many mourners in attendance. William Wentworth had been buried on the Wentworth estate, and only family and a few close friends had attended. William's widow, Georgiana, had sold her late husband's interest in the shipping business, and she returned to England shortly afterward, leaving Margaret Ann in the care of Irene Kent.

Martha Huntington Gage had to bear the absence of her beloved son, who was now residing and working as a physician in Cambridge. Joshua Pierce was serving hard time in a prison, subjected to harsh treatment and conditions. Gordon Conroy, a former sergeant stripped of his rank for inappropriate behavior and other unlawful acts, was serving as a colonial working in the vast and dangerous wilderness, building homes for new settlers under the watchful eye of the militia.

Irene Kent although sadden by her brother William's crimes and his tragic death, knew that life must go on, so she focused nearly all of her attention on her niece Margaret Ann, ensuring that the young woman would have a good life. As far as Irene was concerned, the secret of Margaret Ann's parentage died with William Wentworth and General Wolfe. At the present, Irene was busy transforming Black Crow into a civilized, well-mannered, and accomplished gentleman who would make the perfect suitor and protector for Margaret Ann with no one suspecting that he was a Huron warrior. Since Irene's husband, General Kent, and their son, Cooper, had returned temporarily to England with the general's army, she had the luxury of carrying out her plan, which was proving to be very successful, even to her astonishment.

As people were celebrating, Richard Hayes hurried his way through the busy streets while on his way to the Governor's Mansion, a white frame building with yellow shutters and a gilded roof resembling a dome, which faced the town square. Upon his arrival, he had upset the entire household and broke all rules of protocol by insisting on seeing the governor at once.

Governor Fenton was about to sit down to dinner, but he surprised his servants and his wife by ordering his cook to postpone the meal.

He received Richard in his library. After extending congratulations and gratitude for Richard's bravery in bringing certain unscrupulous and dangerous scoundrels to justice, the governor sat down at his desk and motioned for his visitor to take a seat.

"I was going to send for you in the next day or two, Major Hayes, but you have saved me the trouble," he said. "I have just learned that Theodore Blakeslee's home has been sold, as well as his personal belongings, and that some of the money he had swindled from you and your associates has been recovered. I am having the necessary papers prepared to confiscate those funds on behalf of the Crown."

Richard listened attentively as the governor continued to speak.

"I am sorry to say that Theodore Blakeslee spent money as fast as it came in to him. I'm afraid that you will not be able to recover all of your losses. However, five thousand pounds is remaining. How much do you need to settle your debt?"

"Three thousand pounds for my friends and associates, Your Excellency, and two thousand pounds for myself," said a humble Richard. "I will send three thousand to London, and clear my name with the King's Criminal Court. Whatever is left over will be more than enough to buy some property and begin a new life."

"I'll send a letter to London myself in order to expedite matters there," replied a smiling Governor Fenton. "But I'm afraid that two thousand pounds will not buy you much in the way of a house and land in England."

"I have no intention of returning to England," said Richard. "I hope to remain in America. But I will need help in accomplishing my purpose."

The governor listened intently to Richard while tapping the table with his forefinger. Then he made Richard an inviting offer.

"I am delighted you are going to remain here. It so happens that the colony is intending to open up a new section of the wilderness to settlement in the next month. We will need to establish a company of militia out there to be made up of men who will build homes and farms in the region. The western frontier is a sensitive but also untamed area these days, so I am hoping to recruit experienced and brave individuals to provide the necessary backbone. Of course, I'll need an experienced officer in charge, and I would be pleased to offer you command of the company, major. And also, as a special incentive, the colony will offer you two hundred acres, free of charge. Do you accept my offer?"

"I accept your offer with humbleness and gratitude. I will do my best to do right by the settlement, its settlers, and the colonists of this colony as well as Your Excellency," said Richard as he reached his hand out to the governor.

"And, one last request. My wife and I are hosting a ball tomorrow night here at the mansion, and your presence is greatly requested. Also, my wife has informed me that a young lady by the name of Sarah Dustin was invited, but she is in need of an escort. Would you happen to know of an eligible gentleman who would like to escort the young lady?" smiled Governor Fenton.

"Tell your wife that I will attend the ball and that Miss Dustin will have an escort," said Richard.

After sealing their agreement with a firm handshake, an elated Richard left the Governor's Mansion and ran through the streets, joining in the festivities. In the vicinity nearby, a fife and drum corps was playing music with more enthusiasm than skill. Every church bell in the city was ringing, and with each passing minute still more people seemed to appear in the streets, cheering and clapping as the soldiers marched by.

As he was partaking in the celebrations with the local colonists, Richard caught a glimpse of a gold ring on the finger of a tradesman standing next to him. As the sunlight glistened upon the ring, Richard remembered what George Dustin had told him about the gold medallion and its supposed curse. After thinking about all that had taken place and the fact that Theodore was dead and Sarah was safe, he believed that there was no need to think about the medallion. Theodore's wicked deeds died with him, so Richard decided to forget about the medallion and hoped that it would stay forgotten.

---

Governor Fenton informed the cook to proceed with the meal. While he waited, the governor began to write the letter he had promised Richard he would send to London to clear his name. He was relieved that Richard had not mentioned the gold medallion that had been found in Theodore's pocket after he had died. Opening a desk drawer, Governor Fenton stared at the shiny and mysterious object. Suddenly, his eyes began to hurt, so he closed the drawer and locked the desk. He sat back in his chair and closed his eyes for a few moments. Then he continued writing the letter. But he was unaware that Lord Amherst was watching him from outside the library window.

# Chapter 28

The night of the ball had arrived. Fancy horse-drawn carriages took turns lining up at the entrance of the Governor's Mansion. Footmen dressed in powdered wigs and tailored suits held flaming torches that provided light for the arriving guests. Several footmen assisted the women out of the carriages. Inside the great hall, musicians played lively music while elegantly dressed men and women filled the room with conversation, dancing, drinking, and celebrating. Governor and Mrs. Fenton played the dutiful host and hostess by greeting all the guests upon their arrival. Many members of Boston's high society were in attendance, as well as prominent businessmen, merchants, tradesmen, and high-ranking officers.

Sitting in a corner was Martha Huntington Gage, fanning herself and watching her son, Thomas, talking with a group of young ladies and officers. Martha was delighted that Thomas had returned home for a short stay and had escorted his mother to the ball. Thomas seemed healthy and very content, which gave much comfort to Martha. Like most mothers, Martha was satisfied when her children were happy. She did wish for a visit from her daughter, Cassandra, and her son-in-law, who were living in England. Although she still longed for the day when Thomas would take a wife and fill Huntington Hall with children, Martha was willing to accept his present status as a physician and bachelor while waiting patiently for the latter to happen.

Mabel Dustin did not attend the ball, for she believed it to be too soon since the passing of her husband, George. She was content remaining at home in her drawing room, sipping tea and reading the Bible, which brought her solace, particularly during this time of mourning. However, Mabel gave her blessing and permission for Sarah to attend the ball with Richard Hayes. She knew that her daughter was safe and in wonderful company with the major. Sarah desperately needed to get out and be among people, and the ball provided a perfect opportunity.

Sarah wore a green gown with fancy lace and a pearl necklace that had been a gift from her father. Richard looked strikingly handsome in his scarlet and white officer's uniform. He and Sarah made a handsome couple who received the attention of many guests, who admired their fine features.

One of the last guests to arrive was Irene Kent, who always fancied herself and could be counted upon for making a grand entrance. However, Irene was not the only one who would capture the attention of an entire audience that evening.

Irene was dressed in a fine velvet gown with lace trim as well as diamond earrings and matching necklace. She was accompanied by a very handsome couple. The gentleman was wearing a tailored suit. He had broad shoulders, dark brown eyes, and luscious black hair tied neatly in the back with a ribbon. He certainly received the attention of the ladies present, including Mrs. Fenton. The lovely young lady who was with him was dressed in a beautiful satin gown and a ruby necklace around her neck. Her dark hair and shiny blue eyes added to her beauty.

A proud Irene introduced the good-looking couple to Governor and Mrs. Fenton.

"Governor and Mrs. Fenton, let me introduce you to my niece, Margaret Ann Thatcher, and her companion, Bradley Cross. Mr. Cross is an acquaintance of General Kent's and is from a respected family from the north of England," said Irene.

"It is a pleasure to meet you both. Please, go in and enjoy the celebration," said the governor with a smile.

Margaret Ann and Bradley went into the great hall while Irene remained behind. Mrs. Fenton commented that Margaret Ann and Bradley were a fine-looking couple, but also added that Bradley's complexion appeared a bit tan.

Irene quickly responded to the woman's rude and inquisitive remark.

"He has done extensive traveling recently, and his skin has been exposed to the sun. He has a fortune of ten thousand pounds a year. I do believe it will be a terrific match between him and my niece, and for both our families," said a calm and complacent Irene.

"Indeed it shall, my dear Irene. Families are inherited, and relationships are earned, and I do think their relationship is worth every pound," laughed Governor Fenton.

Irene agreed with the governor and then graciously took her leave. As she walked away, Irene chuckled to herself, because only Margaret Ann and she knew that Bradley Cross was really Black Crow.

Once all the guests had arrived, Governor and Mrs. Fenton entered the reception hall. The musicians stopped playing, and Governor Fenton began to speak. He thanked everyone for attending, and after the servants distributed champagne glasses to all the guests, he proposed a toast to the end of the war and the prosperity of all of England's colonies, especially Massachusetts Bay.

Following the toast, several of the guests lined up and waited patiently for the music to start playing. The governor and his wife led the group in the minuet, which was a popular dance in England and the colonies. Sarah and Richard also danced the minuet. Margaret Ann and Bradley stood off to the side, sipping punch and watching the activities. Many young ladies in the crowd envied Margaret Ann and tried with strong desperation to control themselves from walking up to Bradley and touching his black hair.

Irene had done a magnificent job of transforming a wild savage into a well-mannered and sophisticated gentleman. As always, Black Crow remained attentive and protective of Margaret Ann. He smiled pleasantly, did not speak very often, and held his head up high without ever faltering or giving away his true identity.

Although Irene's husband, General Kent, was not present, she had a grand time at the ball, particularly when she observed the happy expression on her niece's face. Irene knew deep down in her heart that the relationship Margaret Ann wanted with Black Crow was forbidden by society and the charade would only last for so long. Thomas Gage had a suspicion that Brandon Cross was Black Crow since he was acquainted with him. However, Thomas remained silent as he lifted his left brow in approval when staring at Irene from across the ballroom. Irene appreciated Thomas's silence. For the present, she would partake in her niece's happiness as long as Margaret Ann and Black Crow kept their part of the deal they made with Irene that Black Crow was to be Margaret Ann's companion and protector, and not her lover. Irene planned on keeping a very close watch on them while worrying about what could transpire for another time.

Martha approached Irene and complimented her. While they were talking, Thomas joined them and began telling Irene about his work at the hospital in Cambridge, which interested her very much.

When the minuet was finished, Mrs. Fenton made her way about the room, speaking to her guests. Governor Fenton approached Irene's cozy little group. He shook Thomas's hand and congratulated him on the good work he was doing in Cambridge. Martha remarked how well Sarah and Margaret Ann looked, and also admired both of their partners. Irene smiled with satisfaction.

"What a magnificent gathering of such fine people! We all have something to celebrate as apparent on the many smiling faces in this room," said Martha.

"Yes, indeed it is," said Irene. "And we have much to celebrate with the war ended and many of us putting our lives back together after these trying and tragic few months. There is much laughter, happiness, and good people all around us. But most of all, there is love in this room. It is love that shall sustain us through prosperous and difficult times."

After Irene had finished speaking, everyone in the group agreed with her, and Governor Fenton called for another toast.

A servant had gone to open the terrace doors to let in a cool evening breeze that was a welcome relief to several of the guests. As all those in the great hall celebrated, outside on the terrace, hidden in the shadows, Lord Jeffrey Amherst was watching surreptitiously. He cautiously made his way to the terrace doors, where he spied on the guests talking, laughing, and dancing. With his eyes concealed behind a black mask, he looked about the great hall and then finally saw the beautiful Margaret Ann, who was preoccupied with her tall and handsome companion.

After staring for some time, Lord Amherst whispered, "One day soon you shall be mine, my lovely Margaret Ann. But for now, I shall bide my time." And then he slowly faded into the darkness while laughing nefariously to himself.